ROMANCING MELODY

A CROSSING JOURNEY

CARRIE DAWS

IMMEASURABLE
WORKS

ROMANCING MELODY

© 2013 by Carrie Daws

Printed in the United States of America

ISBN: 978-0-9981678-4-8

eISBN: 978-0-9981678-5-5

Cover design by Hannah Stanley

Page Layout by Carrie Daws

For baby Jacob
and his brave parents

Hear, O Lord, and answer me,
For I am poor and needy.
Guard my life, for I am devoted to You.
You are my God; save your servant
Who trusts in You.
Have mercy on me, O Lord,
For I call to You all day long.
Bring joy to your servant,
For to You, O Lord,
I lift up my soul.

Psalm 86:1-4

CHAPTER 1

$\mathcal{T}$HE CONTRACTION SURPRISED 21-year-old Melody Podell, and she almost dropped her glass. The water sloshed as she slammed the glass onto the table and grabbed the chair for support. Breathing through the pain, she looked at the digital reading on the microwave. 5:37pm. *Third contraction in less than an hour,* she thought, *and this one was a lot stronger. I'd better sit for a while. David will be home soon.*

Comfortably propped on the couch, she twisted her long, dark brown hair into a bun and held it on top of her head with one hand while fanning herself with a folded copy of the May 9th edition of *The Army Times*. Predictions for a busier than usual hurricane season for the Atlantic filled the evening news.

And Mom thought Fayetteville, North Carolina, would be a safe place. I suppose it is, minus the late summer hurricanes.

Feeling her stomach tightening, she looked at the wall clock. 5:50. *Maybe that clock is off a few minutes from the microwave.*

As she breathed through the end of another contraction

ten minutes later, she reached for the phone. *No answer at work. David must be on his way home. No reason to panic. It's probably just Braxton-Hicks.*

AT 9:52PM THE PHONE RANG IN THE NEONATAL INTENSIVE Care Unit at Womack Army Medical Center on Fort Bragg, North Carolina, and Sara reached for it.

"Thirty-five weeker came into the ER in heavy labor. She's on her way up to Labor and Delivery. We'll need a NICU team."

"Be right there." Sara hung up the phone, removed her reading glasses, and looked at her supervisor. "Thirty-five weeker. We need a team to L and D."

"Okay," her supervisor said. "Wanna take it?"

Sara walked down the hall thinking through her night. Thirty-two years on the job had taught her to take advantage of every quiet moment, even if they were while she moved from one station to the next.

The Rovack baby's lungs are doing a little better, she thought. *But I'll bet he needs another dose of surfactant. Wonder if McKendrick will head to surgery tonight?* She checked the time on her small wristwatch. *The redness on his abdomen is definitely more pronounced than when I worked Tuesday. Scavetta is rooming in tonight and should discharge in the morning. That will put us down to nine babies before this new one. Thirty-five weeks, though. He shouldn't be a problem.*

CHAPTER 2

*M*ELODY LURCHED FORWARD IN BED, sitting up with her hand to her chest. Her heart raced as she pushed her hair behind her ears and tried to take deep breaths. The dream remained fresh in her mind, propelling her down the hall to four-month-old Cole's nursery.

Gently pushing open his door, she held her breath as she watched in the soft glow of the froggy nightlight, allowing the movement of her baby's chest to reassure her. His lips puckered briefly and relaxed again as he moved an arm out beside him.

She silently crossed the plush tan carpet to stand at the crib side. Her precious Cole. How close they'd come to losing him. Her mind still clearly remembered all the wires coming out of his small body. His birth at 35-weeks had surprised both her and her husband, David, but labor seemed to go well.

Until Cole came out. Underdeveloped lungs. Surfactant. Broad spectrum antibiotics. The medical terms circled in her head and invaded her sleep. The scary hours as her boy was intubated and she could hardly pull herself from his bedside.

The tears she'd shed when the nurses finally extubated him and she watched him take those wonderful breaths on his own. The days spent in the hospital as he gained the strength to come home.

Pull yourself together, Melody. Doctor Braddock said Cole is looking great. His check-up went smoothly last Thursday. There's nothing to worry about.

She moved to the glider just a few feet from the crib and sat down, looking at the mobile hanging above Cole's peach-fuzz covered head. David had fallen in love with the cute frogs and snails, declaring it the perfect design for a boy. "After all," he'd said in his deep southern drawl, "boys are made from frogs, snails, and puppy-dog tails."

I'm just missing David, she thought. *What a rotten time for a deployment.*

He'd left with his team on August 29, and she expected him to be gone just over four months. He'd worked hard to earn his place in a Special Forces unit at Fort Bragg, and she didn't want to put his career in jeopardy. *SpecOps is his dream. I can't ask him to walk away.*

But her heart was torn. *How is a marriage supposed to survive this life? Between deployments and training, he's gone more than half the year. He'll miss Cole's first tooth, learning to roll over, maybe his first steps. How am I supposed to do this by myself? Doesn't a boy need his father?*

Sighing deeply, Melody stood to look at Cole one final time before heading back to bed. Maybe this time her dreams wouldn't center on those horrible eight days in the NICU.

MELODY FELT GUILTY DROPPING COLE OFF AT THE CHILD Development Center Friday morning. The free childcare offered to spouses of deployed soldiers was nice, but Cole was still so young. She paused outside the door, almost turning around to go back for her son, when her phone vibrated.

"Still coming?" the text read.

Melody sighed deeply. *Lunch will be a nice treat. I'm not being selfish. I'm taking a break so that I can be a better mom. Cole is safe. And it's only for three hours.* She repeated the well-rehearsed speech in her mind as she typed out a reply to her friend. "On the way."

"LOOK AT MY HANDSOME BOY AWAKE FROM HIS AFTERNOON nap." Melody leaned over the crib, smiling at her son. She tickled his belly, looking for his usual quick grin. His blue eyes, so like his father's, just peered back at her.

"My goodness, your nose is runny. Is that why you're slow to smile today? Let's get you cleaned up." She laid him gently on the changing table to check his diaper and clean his nose.

"Now where did you catch this?" Melody thought back. *The CDC was a week ago.* He squirmed at the nasal aspirator but was soon breathing more clearly. *Maybe the commissary this morning? How long does it take to catch a cold, anyway?*

She stood him up to face her, allowing him a moment to push against the table with his feet.

"Are you ready to eat?" Melody smiled at him, moving in closer to rub her nose against Cole's. He bounced, smiling at her and cooing in response. "Oh, yeah? You're ready to eat?"

Melody moved in again to rub noses with him and real-ized as she picked him up that her nose was a little wet. She looked again at Cole and grabbed a tissue. "Looks like you might have caught a cold, baby boy."

Settling in the glider, Melody positioned a pillow to

support Cole while he latched onto her. Rubbing his head gently, she said, "I think we'll just stay home the next couple of days while you get over it. Not like we had someplace to go, anyway."

MELODY APPROACHED THE FRONT DOORS TO ROCKFISH Church on Sunday morning, looking at every person within view.

She has to be here today. Please, God, let her be here.

The greeters held open the glass doors for the crowd exiting from the first service. Melody navigated the crowd entering for the second service, carrying the car seat with Cole safely buckled inside it.

The full foyer overwhelmed her for a moment, but then, finally, she saw the wonderful NICU nurse who had helped her understand everything that had happened at the hospital. Pushing through the crowd, she called out, "Sara! Can I ask you a question?"

Sara turned her head from the lady she was talking to. "Hey, Melody! What's up?"

"I know you're off duty and all..."

"Is everything okay with Cole?"

"No. Well, maybe. I... I'm just not sure." Melody looked at Sara, tears beginning to mist her eyes.

Sara stepped closer and touched Melody's arm. "Come on. Let's go talk."

Sara led Melody to the reception office, the first door down the hallway. Melody put the carrier down on the cushioned chair as a tear fell down her cheek.

"I'm sorry. I'm probably overreacting. It's just with David gone and my mom so far away..."

Sara reached to the desk behind her and grabbed the box of tissues. "It's okay, Melody. I don't mind helping."

"He's just had this runny nose since Thursday afternoon. And now he doesn't seem to be interested in eating much. I mean, he's still eating, but not like he used to."

"Let's take a look, okay?"

Melody nodded, and Sara reached for the carrier. Putting the handle down, she pulled the light blanket away and looked at Cole.

"You do have a runny nose there, kiddo." Sara felt his head. "Have you noticed any kind of fever?" Sara grabbed a tissue to wipe Cole's nose.

"Sometimes. It's like 99.2 or close to that. I think the highest has been 99.4."

"He seems to be a little warm right now, but that could just be because it's still plenty warm outside. I think autumn forgot to tell October to cool down a bit."

Melody smiled as she dabbed at her tears with a fresh tissue.

"When's the last time he was in for a well-baby check-up?"

"About two and a half weeks ago."

"And that went okay?"

Melody nodded.

"It's probably just a cold. Keep an eye on him for the next day or two, and if he doesn't get better, or if his appetite continues to decrease, take him in to see his doctor."

CHAPTER 3

"*M*om, I just don't know what to do for him."
Melody sniffed and wiped at the tears again.

"Did you try a humidifier in his room? Or a warm bath?"

Melody nodded before speaking into the receiver, imagining her mom's slight frame stood before her instead of 2,800 miles away. "I tried the humidifier, but his cold just seems to be getting worse. Now he's coughing, and his fever is climbing."

"What's his temperature?"

"It's hanging around 100.5."

"Oh, sweetie, I'm sure it's nothing. It could just be teething. Lots of babies get a temperature right before a tooth pops through. He's almost five months, so that first tooth should be making an appearance any time now."

"You think so, Mom?"

"You said Sara wasn't concerned yesterday, right?"

"Yeah." Melody peeked in Cole's room and watched him sleep. Was it just her imagination, or was he breathing faster?

"As long as he's still eating, I would wait another couple

of days. If you don't see a tooth by Wednesday, or if his fever hits 101, then you should take him in."

"I wish you were here, Mom."

"Me, too, sweetie."

"MRS. PODELL?"

Melody looked up from where she sat in the waiting room, struggling to hold Cole. She stood, grabbed the infant carrier, and followed the nurse in the happy-colored, kid-friendly scrubs down the short hall to a room.

"Come on in, Mrs. Podell, and have a seat. You called this morning to say Cole is sick?" The nurse blew a puff of air upwards, sending her bangs away from her eyes, but the errant red locks fell back in almost the same position.

"Yes. It started with a runny nose, and then a low fever developed." Cole twisted his head in her arms to look at the nurse. "The fever's been going up, and now he's not really wanting to eat much."

The nurse logged into the computer beside Melody and clicked on Cole's chart. Cole rubbed his face on Melody's chest and turned his head to look out the door.

"When did all this start?" The nurse reached out to feel Cole's fuzzy head.

"The runny nose started last Thursday."

The nurse typed a few notes. "Six days. What about the fever?"

"I started checking him on Friday, but it was only about ninety-nine then. By Saturday night, it had climbed just a little, not even a half a point, though. And by Monday morning, it was just over a hundred."

"All right." The nurse typed a few more quick notes. "And when did you notice a change in his eating habits?"

Cole squirmed, so Melody turned him around to face the nurse. He quickly reached around for Melody, and she turned him sideways on her lap. He looked back at the nurse and then laid his head against Melody.

"I guess a little on Friday, but more so yesterday. Last night he didn't eat much at all before bed, and during the night he really didn't seem to want much."

"How much would you say he's eaten today?"

Melody squeezed him gently to her. "I'm not real good at saying. He's still breast feeding, and I can't really tell."

"Not a problem. How about this? How often does he normally feed and for how long?"

"About every three hours for 25 to 30 minutes."

"And today?"

"I keep trying every hour or two because he's been fussy, but he's only latched on a couple times, and then only for five or ten minutes."

The nurse watched Cole for a moment, calmly lying against Melody. "He definitely doesn't look like he feels good."

"Do you think it's just teething?"

The nurse smiled at her. "I'm sure it's something just that simple. Let me get his temperature and weight; then I'll finalize these notes to Cole's chart. Dr. Braddock's running just a bit behind this afternoon, but it shouldn't be too long."

MELODY HELD COLE CLOSE. AFTER THE NURSE FINISHED, HE had snuggled into Melody and fallen asleep. Now, twenty minutes later, fear was setting into Melody's mind once again. *What if this isn't just a cold? What if they send him to the hospital? Can I get ahold of David? Should I even tell him?*

Melody began to rock slightly. *David needs to focus on his job. I can't distract him. But what if this is serious? How bad does it have to be for the Army to send him home?*

"Mrs. Podell, I'm sorry to keep you waiting." Dr. Braddock closed the door behind him and washed his hands. "I see my patient fell asleep on me."

He sat down at the computer and read the few notes the nurse had taken and then turned around to face Cole. "Well, his temperature is definitely a bit higher than I'd like. Other than not eating, what else have you noticed?"

"He's been grumpy and not sleeping well. He'll sleep for an hour or so and then wake up for awhile. Even at night."

Cole coughed.

"When did the cough start?"

Melody sighed as she tried to remember. "I'm not sure. Sunday afternoon, maybe. Or maybe Saturday night. I, I just..." Tears began gathering.

"It's okay, Mrs. Podell. Don't stress over your answer. Let me just take a listen to those lungs of his."

Melody shifted in her seat so that Cole's weight fell more against her as she removed her arm from his back to give the doctor access. She watched him move the stethoscope around and turn to make some notes in the computer. *He's just being thorough. Nothing is horribly wrong with my baby.*

"I'm going to take a look in his ears too." He reached for the instruments hanging against the wall and a disposable cover. After he finished with the ear facing outward, Melody gently turned Cole's head to give Dr. Braddock access to his left side. He turned back to the computer to make a few more notes as Melody nervously began rocking Cole.

"Okay. I can tell you definitively that Cole has an ear infection in his right ear. He seems to be working hard to breathe, and while I don't hear noise in his lungs, the air doesn't sound as free as it should be. Congestion, runny nose, cough—that's all obvious. This is probably just an early winter cold, but I want to run a couple of simple tests to make sure, okay?"

Melody nodded.

"Am I remembering correctly that your husband is on active duty?"

"Yes." Melody barely squeaked out the word.

"Is he home?"

"No, sir. He just left a little over a month ago."

Dr. Braddock nodded. "Afghanistan?"

Melody nodded.

"How long will he be gone?"

"About four months."

"Well. I'm sure all this will be well behind you by the time he gets home." He turned back to the computer. "I'm putting in a prescription for amoxicillin. I want you to start Cole on it as soon as you possibly can and give him a dose every six hours. I know you're not going to want to wake him if he's sleeping, but it's really important that he gets this as close to that six-hour schedule as possible."

"Okay." Melody swallowed. *Amoxicillin. I can handle that.*

"Any questions for me?"

"I don't think so."

"All right then. Before you leave, I'm going to send the nurse back in. We'll have you out of here in just a few minutes."

Melody nodded. As the doctor walked out, she held Cole closer. He seemed to sleep better sitting up with her. "Maybe we should try sleeping in the recliner tonight, sweet boy," she whispered above his head.

A moment later, the nurse whisked back into the room with a small tray. "Well, he seems to be sleeping all right for now. You know, with that ear infection, he'll probably be more comfortable propped up than lying on his back."

"Okay. We'll try that."

"I just need to get a nasal sample, and you'll be good to go." She held up a culture swab. "If you'll just hold him still, I'll get a little bit from what's runnin', and he won't notice a thing."

The nurse took her sample and handed Melody a tissue to wipe the rest from Cole's upper lip. "Your prescription has already been called in, so you can stop on your way home. This will head to the lab tonight, and Dr. Braddock will call you tomorrow if there's anything to be concerned about."

"HE'S SLEEPING RIGHT NOW, MOM. I STUFFED A COUPLE OF pillows and a thick blanket under one end of his mattress so it's at more of an angle for him."

"The doctor just thinks it's an ear infection?"

"Yeah, and probably a cold. The nurse said he'd call if the tests turned up anything."

"Well, good. Are you going to tell David about it?"

"I'll probably just tell him about the ear infection. I don't want him to worry."

"What if the tests come back with something?"

"I'll deal with that then. It's not like he can call regularly. He's not at any of the bases."

"I thought he was in Mazari Sharif?"

"No, Mom. He just flew into there. I can't really talk about it on the phone. Remember OpSec."

"That's the security stuff, right?"

"Yes. Operational security. I can't discuss where he's gone, what he's doing, or when he'll be home over any telephone line, including the Internet." *Not that I really know that much anyway*, Melody thought. David's job as weapons sergeant with the 3rd Special Forces Group brought with it quite a bit of secrecy. And not being raised around a military base,

Melody was still trying to figure out the basics, like if a brigade was bigger than a battalion or vice versa.

Melody heard her mom sigh. "I don't think I'll ever understand all those acronyms."

"Me either, Mom."

CHAPTER 4

"COLE, YOU HAVE TO EAT, BABY." Melody tried to hold back the frustration as tears lined her lower eyelids. The little sleep he'd gotten over night had been fitful, and his eating had continued to decrease. He struggled to sit up, so she lowered her shirt and held him close. He nestled against her shoulder.

"I know you don't feel good, sweetheart." She rubbed his head gently, rocking in the glider in Cole's room. Her phone vibrating against the changing table interrupted the peaceful moment.

"Hello?" She sandwiched the phone between her ear and shoulder so she could securely hold Cole.

"Mrs. Podell? This is Dr. Braddock."

Melody's heartbeat seemed to speed up as a lump formed in her throat.

"I have the test results back from Cole's culture, and I have some concerns. How quickly can you get him to the hospital?"

Melody's mind raced. *Hospital?* "Uh, we could leave in just a few minutes."

"Great. Will you be going to Womack?"

"Y-yes."

"I'm going to call in some orders to Pediatrics, so when you get there, don't bother checking into the ER. Just go straight to the third floor. Got it?"

"Okay." Melody hung up the phone and hugged Cole tightly. *Third floor.* She walked to the diaper bag and quickly examined its contents, adding a few diapers. *I wonder how long we'll be. Is Cole being admitted?* Sigh. *I should have asked that. He said get there quickly.* She laid Cole down in his crib and grabbed two more diapers and a pair of jammies to stuff in the diaper bag before rushing to get her shoes.

SARA EXITED THE ELEVATOR AND WALKED DOWN THE HALL toward the front entrance of the hospital. Her afternoon on the town with her husband had been interrupted by a call from the NICU to come in to sign a form on a child she'd worked with two nights before. They needed it done before she'd be back on shift in three days. She smiled as she thought about her spouse patiently waiting in the truck out front to start their afternoon with lunch at their favorite restaurant.

As she rounded the corner, she looked up to see a very disheveled Melody come rushing through the front door. "Melody!"

She watched her jump slightly and then come rushing over. "Sara! Thank God, you're here."

"What's going on, honey?"

"Dr. Braddock called." The tears started running down her cheeks. "He said he had some concerns and needed to run more tests. He told me to report to the Children's Place."

Sara suppressed a smile at Melody's mistake. "Do you know where you are going?"

"No!" The word came out more of a sob than anything. "Third floor is all he said."

"Come on. I'll walk you up to the children's ward." Sara put her arm around Melody and turned her in the right direction. "What tests has he already run?"

"Yesterday he listened to Cole's lungs and had the nurse get some of his snot on one of those big Q-tips."

"Did he tell you what that found?"

"No. He just said to get here quickly."

Sara hit the elevator button and then texted her husband that Melody was at the hospital with Cole. As the doors opened, her nurse mind began to analyze the little bit she was able to glean, and a frightful thought came to her mind: RSV.

Respiratory syncytial virus was common among children, but most breezed through it without their parents knowing anything was seriously wrong. *However, if there are complicating factors—*

Sara stopped herself, remembering her devotions that morning. *2 Corinthians 10:5. I will take every thought captive and make it obedient to Christ. Even the medical ones. But, dear God, what are you doing with this precious child?*

MELODY LOOKED AT HER BABY, TRYING TO CONTROL THE TEARS and understand what the doctor was telling her. RSV. Isolation. IV fluids. Antibiotics. The words ran together and circled in her brain. *Not Cole. They're wrong.*

She felt Sara beside her, heard her asking questions. Cole cried out as the nurse stuck a needle into him. She longed to hold him, comfort him. *It's okay, baby,* she thought. *We'll be home soon. This won't be like last time. We won't be here for long.*

"Thank you, doctor," said Sara. "Melody?"

Melody ripped her gaze from her child and looked at Sara. Tears streaked her face. She raised a shaking hand to push a strand of hair behind her ear. "I don't understand. He was doing good. The doctor said he was fine. I thought we were past all this."

Sara grabbed her hand and led her to a chair, sitting beside her. "Melody, you didn't do anything wrong. The doctor didn't do anything wrong. Lots of kids get RSV. It's very common, and these doctors and nurses deal with it a lot."

Melody looked at her child, still whimpering as the nurses worked on him. "Did they have to put the IV in?"

"He's dehydrated and needs the fluids. Plus, the antibiotics they'll be able to give him through the IV will absorb better into his system than anything oral. It will help him feel better faster."

Melody nodded her head. *How am I going to explain all this to David? He doesn't even know Cole is sick yet. Will I even be able to talk to him?*

"What can I do?" said Sara. "Do you want some lunch?"

"No." The thought of food made her queasy.

"Can I call anyone? Do you want anyone at church to know?"

Melody's mind flooded with emotion. *Mom needs to know, but I should call her. What about David?*

"How long do you think Cole will be here, Sara?" *Maybe if it's just a day or two, David won't need to know until it's over.*

"The fluids should work pretty quick, so it's really a matter of how fast he responds to the medicine. I would say at least a couple of days, but they'll know more tomorrow."

A couple of days. Will David try to call? Who else might he try if he can't reach me? Melody's mind sorted through different faces at church, but the truth was they hadn't connected with anyone. They showed up on Sunday morning just before service started and left right after. She wasn't even sure how to call the church.

"I can add Cole to the prayer list." Sara looked at her expectantly.

"Yes, please." *It certainly can't hurt.*

MELODY WOKE DURING THE NIGHT AS THE NURSE CAME IN TO check Cole's vitals. She sat up and watched the short woman work, her head barely visible above the top of the bars on Cole's crib. She looked at the monitors and made a few notations before pulling out a notepad. Then she grabbed her stethoscope and gently placed it on his chest. Melody watched her expression change.

"Is everything okay? Is he doing better?"

The nurse looked at her. "Did the doctor do any x-rays?"

"I don't think so. We came straight up here, and Cole hasn't left this room since."

"I'm going to talk to the doctor. I think we need to get a look at what's going on in these lungs of his."

Melody's throat restricted. She balled her fists around the thin hospital blanket provided to her. "Is he worse?"

"Nothing we weren't expecting, Mrs. Podell. Pneumonia is a natural progression for RSV. I'm sure it's nothing to be overly concerned about."

Natural progression? Not be overly concerned? Melody tried to breath deeply. These nurses saw this all the time. Every day kids got sick, and every day kids got better. *Cole just needs a little more time for the medicine to work. That's all. Just a little more time.*

CHAPTER 5

"*M*RS. PODELL?"

Melody turned in her chair where she kept watch over Cole. "Yes?"

"I'm a doctor with the Pediatric ICU." He adjusted the wire-rimmed glasses on his long nose. "We're going to be taking over your baby's care."

Melody stood and grabbed onto the edge of the crib, instantly afraid of what this meant. "Why? What's wrong?"

"His x-rays show that he does have pneumonia. His temperature went up overnight, and his breathing became more shallow. Even with the antibiotics in his system, he has continued to get sicker. The x-rays also showed his heart is enlarged..."

The doctor continued talking, but Melody's mind froze on the three phrases she understood. *ICU. Getting sicker. Heart is enlarged.* She looked at her precious baby. *David! I don't know what to do.* Tears filled her eyes, and she felt her legs getting weak.

"Mrs. Podell?" The doctor was suddenly beside her. "Have a seat. I know this is a lot to absorb. The nurses will get Cole transferred to the PICU, and someone will come walk you through all the procedures, visiting hours and such. Do you have any questions?"

Questions? Why does everyone keep asking me if I have any questions? I just want to go home. I just want to take my baby home. A sob escaped her as she covered her mouth with her hand. *How am I going to tell David?*

MELODY WALKED IN HER FRONT DOOR LATER THAT EVENING. She dropped her purse and Cole's diaper bag at the front door and stumbled back to his room. She barely made it to the glider before succumbing to another bout of tears.

When she was forced out of the PICU at the end of visiting hours, she turned her cell phone on to find she'd missed David's call. The doctors were busy running tests but weren't yet sure what was wrong with Cole's heart. The antibiotics were flooding his system but didn't seem to be helping the pneumonia.

She leaned her head against the back of the chair and closed her eyes.

Melody. I am here.

The voice was so clear that her eyes flew open, and she looked around the room. All the shadows seemed to belong. "Who's there?"

The silence overwhelmed her. She flew to the door and turned on the light, spinning to look around the room again. Seeing nothing, she turned and looked down the hall. Listening carefully but hearing nothing, she shook her head. "I'm just tired. That's all."

She took one more look around the room, turned off the light, and walked back to the front door to pick up her cell phone. Desperate to talk to someone, she brought up her contacts.

The person at the top of her contacts list was Brittany Griffin, the oncology nurse she used to work with at Doernbecher Children's Hospital in Portland, Oregon. "I haven't talked to Brittney in over a year."

She'd attended Brittney's wedding shortly before Brittney had transferred from the hospital to the clinic in Crossing, just a short drive from Portland. They'd seen each other a few times after that, including at her own wedding to David. *Interesting that Brittany's husband and David were high school best friends.*

"Brittany used to talk to God a lot. And she'd understand all the medical stuff. Maybe she'd be a good person to talk to."

She started to dial but then stopped. *What is she going to think about me calling after all these months?*

Call, precious one.

Melody looked up again. Was she so tired that she was hearing voices? Looking around and seeing no one, she cautiously touched Brittany's number and let the phone dial.

RYAN GRIFFIN DOUBLE-CHECKED ALL THE LIGHTS BEFORE walking back to the front desk. The clinic in Crossing, Oregon, was ready to lock up as soon as Brittany finished in the bathroom. Again. Morning sickness was not treating her well. In the two and a half years they'd been married, she'd rarely had so much as a cold, so her being sick was a new experience.

"Are you still praying this eases up before the end of the first trimester?"

He smiled at his wife, who dutifully held up the wall

beside the bathroom door, her dark hair twisted around and held firmly in one hand.

"Yes, ma'am."

"So this should stop sometime in the next five weeks?"

His eyes and brain automatically looked over her carefully due to his years as an EMT on an ambulance and his more recent medical training as he worked towards becoming a physician's assistant. *She really looks pitiful.* "Assuming God says yes."

She rolled her brown eyes. "Ugh. That is not the answer I wanted."

He started towards her. "Well, my beauty..."

She suddenly held up her hand to him. "Hold that thought!"

Ryan sighed as he watched her dart back into the bathroom and slam the door. Hearing her phone, he walked back to the pile waiting near the front door. "Hello, Brittany's phone."

"Umm, hi. Is...uh, is Brittany there?"

He ran a hand through his dark hair. "She can't come to the phone right now. This is her husband. Can I help you?"

"Ryan?"

"Yeah." Ryan leaned against the front counter and crossed one foot over the other. "Who's this?"

"This is Melody. David's wife?" Her voice went up in a question as she wondered whether he would remember her.

"Oh, hey, Mel! How are you? How's David?"

Ryan's tendency to shorten names seemed comforting. It felt familiar, transporting her back to easier days. "David's out of the country right now. He called a couple days ago, so, umm, I'm sure he's fine."

"That's good! When do you expect him home?"

"Not for awhile still."

Ryan paused. *Her attitude isn't matching her words, Father. She's too...somber.* "So what's up? Did you just call to catch up?"

"Uh, yes. Well, no. I..." He heard a deep sigh followed by a quiet sniffle.

Ryan's mind raced. *She said David's fine but out of country. The baby?* "Is Cole okay?"

Ryan heard quiet sobbing. He turned when Brittany touched his arm. He covered the end of the phone with his hand and quietly said, "It's Melody. She's really upset. I think something's going on with Cole, and David's gone."

Brittany nodded as she took the phone from Ryan. "Hey, Melody. It's Brittany."

"Cole's sick." Melody's voice cracked on her son's name as she blurted out the reason for her call, and Brittany tensed up.

"What do you mean, he's sick?"

"He's in the ICU again. They said he's got RSV and pneumonia."

Brittany said a quick prayer for wisdom. "When did he get admitted?"

"Yesterday."

"Well, the doctor has probably started him on antibiotics. You've got to give them time to work."

"They said he's getting sicker, Brittany. They said something's wrong with his heart."

Brittany grabbed Ryan's arm and looked at him. "Did they give you more details than that?"

"Umm, something about his heart being bigger than it's supposed to be. Brittany, I need to know. How bad is that?"

"Melody, I've never worked with infants, so I'm really at a disadvantage here. Do they know why his heart is enlarged?"

"No."

Brittany leaned into Ryan for support as Melody cried. *Daddy, give me words for my friend. What does she need to hear?*

What can I say to her? After a moment she quietly said, "Melody, do you know God loves you?"

Brittany heard Melody's sharp intake of breath. "He loves me? He moved me to the other side of the country, He took my husband and put him in one of the most dangerous places on earth, and now my baby is in the hospital! And you want to tell me that God loves me?"

Brittany's heart broke. "Oh, Mel."

"Look, I know God's been good to you. But not all of us get to work beside our husband and go home every night with him. Some of us have to try to go to sleep wondering if our husband is still alive!"

Brittany stayed quiet, allowing Melody to release her pain.

After a moment, Melody spoke again. "I'm sorry, Brittany. I just, I don't know. I'm just tired. And I feel very alone."

"It's okay," said Brittany. "Can I do anything?"

"Can I call again tomorrow?"

"Girl, you call anytime you want. I'll keep my phone close."

CHAPTER 6

"*M*ELODY?"

Melody jumped as a hand touched her arm. She looked up at the person, trying desperately to focus on the face before her. "Sara?"

"Hey there. How are you doing?"

Melody's eyes watered, and she reached for the tissue box on the floor beside her. "I'm... Well, I'm..." Melody sighed and shook her head, placing the empty tissue box in her lap. "I don't know."

"It's okay."

"Is it?" Melody looked at Sara, then out the window at the room of cribs across from her. Two of the other three cribs in the area were occupied with children of various ages and sizes. She'd watched other moms sitting out in the open with their babies as she sat beside Cole in the relative quiet of the isolation room.

"I'm back at the hospital. David's gone and doesn't even know anything's happening. And every time a nurse comes to check on Cole, I can see it in her face. Something's wrong.

I don't understand all that the doctor is telling me, but I know it's really bad. I just want to go home with my baby, Sara."

Sara crouched down beside her, putting her hand on top of Melody's. "I know you do, honey. Can I help by answering some of your questions? I have to be over in the NICU in a bit, but I came in early to see what I could do for you."

Melody was touched. She missed David checking in on her to see how her day was going. She missed finding love notes in the oddest places and the way he loved to surprise her with a rose or catch her in the middle of the kitchen and begin dancing with her. His romantic pursuit of her had caught her attention in high school and sustained her as she adjusted to being a military spouse. Now, she felt every foot of the geographical distance between them.

"The doctor said his heart is enlarged. What does that mean? Could it be normal for him? What would make a heart grow like that?"

"Well, lots of different things. It could just be the infection he's fighting, or it could be something genetic or a symptom of something more serious. Has the doctor ordered an EKG or an ECHO?"

Melody rubbed her temple, sighing deeply. "I know they've done several different things today, but I can't remember what all they said they were doing. I think EKG was on the list. And they stopped doing his breathing treatments. Won't that make it harder for him to breathe?"

"It might, but they're worried about putting too much stress on his heart. All the medicines we normally use to help the lungs are rough on the heart. The lungs will take longer to heal, but that's a better option right now until they figure out exactly what's going on."

"Sara, I just don't know what to do."

"Keep being a good momma, Melody. Sit here and remind Cole you love him. Ask God to give you understanding about what the doctors are saying..."

Melody began shaking her head.

Sara continued, "...and wisdom on the decisions you make."

"God doesn't care about me, Sara."

"Melody..."

She looked Sara in the eyes. "He doesn't." She looked back at her baby lying in a glass-enclosed crib and shook her head. "He couldn't love me and do this to me."

MELODY PULLED IN HER DRIVEWAY THAT NIGHT AND TURNED off the engine of her 2008 Honda Accord. The world was quiet in their small neighborhood about 25 minutes south of the hospital. No ambulance sirens or beeping pulse oximeters to disturb the peace. She just sat.

David, I need you, she thought. *Do I call you? I know you'd want to know, but if the Army won't let you come home, then you'll just be distracted. Who do I ask to find out if this is bad enough to bring you home?*

Melody looked at her phone as it began vibrating. "Hey, Mom."

"Hey, baby. How are you?"

She rubbed her forehead. "I don't know."

"How's Cole? Did you find out anything new today?"

"He's hanging in there. They stopped his breathing treatments."

"Why?" Melody imagined her mom's eyebrows going up with the sharp question. How she missed the comfort of seeing her mom's face when they talked.

"Sara stopped by before she had to go to work. She said the medicine they use to help the lungs also stresses the heart."

"Oh. I guess you still don't know what's wrong with his heart?"

Fresh tears slipped down her face. She wanted to scream. Her baby's heart was fine. It was just a little big, that's all. He was fine!

"Melody, honey?"

"I'm here, Mom. California just seems so far away."

"What can I do?"

"I don't know. I wish you were here, but all I do is sit in a hospital room. There's no point in you coming for that. I can't even hold him, Mom." She leaned her head back against the seat.

"I'm going to check on airline tickets as soon as we get off the phone, okay?"

Melody sighed. She didn't have the strength to argue one way or the other. Her mom could do nothing here, but wouldn't it be nice to have someone here to walk through this with her? "I love you, Mom."

"I love you too, Melody."

"Do you think Cole knows I love him?"

"I'm sure he does, honey."

"What if he feels abandoned? Lying in that bed feeling miserable. People poking him and wires hanging all over the place. What if he thinks that if this is what life is like, then he doesn't want to get better? Do you think babies think like that, Mom?"

"Ryan Griffin!"

"Mrs. Guire. Can I help you?" The receptionist stood to help the old woman who'd just walked in the door of the clinic in Crossing, Oregon, Monday morning.

"You can find me Ryan Griffin! Or do I need to go knockin' on doors until I find him myself?"

"Now, Mrs. Guire. What's got you all fired up this morning?" Ryan stepped back from the door leading to an examination room to allow his sister, Amber, to walk past him.

Mrs. Guire pointed her finger at Ryan. "You and me got some talkin' to do, boy."

Amber raised her eyebrows as she looked up at Ryan and rubbed her swollen belly. "Four weeks, right?"

"Yeah, Am. Dr. Williams wants to see you back about 28 weeks. Let me know if those headaches get worse or more consistent, and watch your center of balance as it's going to keep changing with the pregnancy."

"Got it. Thanks." Amber turned and walked to the front counter, approaching the woman, who stood at a couple inches less than her own five-foot-two frame. "He's all yours, Mrs. Guire."

"Well?" The woman stood like a fortress in the small waiting area.

Ryan wondered how many people mistook her small stature for weakness. At 66 years of age and roughly 100 pounds, she was quite a character, and people preferred to stay on her good side. Or stay out of her way. "How about you come in here and tell me what's on your mind?"

He followed her back into the examination room, walking over to the exam table to rip off the paper. Wadding it up and tossing it into the wastebasket, he turned to find her still standing. "Would you like to sit here?"

"No. I want to know exactly what is going on with my grand-nephew and why you didn't think it pertinent to inform me immediately."

Ryan put his foot up on the stool at the base of the exam table. "You're grand-nephew?"

"Are you dense, boy?"

"I've been told I'm irritating at times, but I don't think I'm dense."

"Cole. Cole Podell. David and Melody's son."

Everything clicked into place as realization of the family relationships snapped into view. "You're Melody's aunt!"

She pointed her right index finger at him. "I thought we'd established that at her wedding."

"We did, Mrs. Guire. I'm sorry."

"So. Tell me. What's wrong with Cole?"

Ryan shrugged. "I don't really know much, ma'am. Melody called about three nights ago saying he was sick."

"Sick. I would say he's sick. They've moved him to Duke University."

"Duke?" Ryan straightened up. "What happened?"

"That's why I'm here! What do you know about this Duke place?"

Ryan clenched his jaw. "Mrs. Guire, all I know is that Cole was sick with pneumonia, and they suspected something was going on with his heart. The move to Duke tells me that they probably figured out the heart problem and moved him to the best hospital to treat it."

"Would you take your baby there?"

"If I lived in the Southeast, yeah."

"So he's in good hands?"

"Ma'am, all doctors are fallible. We're human. And the body is complex and..."

She stepped forward in the small room and wagged her finger in his face. "Son, I don't need the standard don't-sue-me speech. Is this hospital gonna take good care of my boy or not?"

"I have to believe that they will do their best."

"And if their best ain't good enough?"

"That's what prayers are for, ma'am."

CHAPTER 7

*D*AVID PODELL WIPED HIS BROW as he looked over the Afghanistan landscape. The cold night had given way to temperatures that soared above 100 degrees, and the pounds of protective gear didn't help provide any comfort. *A breeze would be nice, Lord.*

"Podell!"

"Yes, sir!"

"You see something out on those ridges I need to know about?"

David scanned again. "No, sir."

"You got any reason to believe there's something up there to see?"

Other than the fact that we're in Kunar? "No, sir."

Kunar Province definitely included some beautiful landscape, but the hillsides offered great protection to jihadists and smugglers.

"Then get back to work! The guys following us out to this remote location are counting on us having some friendlies to work with."

"Yes, sir!" But as David tried to reach out to any of the villagers willing to talk to him, he kept one eye on the hillsides. Something didn't feel right.

CHAPTER 8

*M*ELODY WALKED IN HER FRONT DOOR after the drive home from Duke University Hospital and leaned against it. She eyed the couch in the living room across from her and then the hallway leading to her bedroom. *I just want to go to sleep and pretend this is all a bad dream.*

She looked at the kitchen refrigerator where her list of home and cell phone numbers for the families of the men her husband deployed with hung. She'd hated that list from the moment David had put it there. "You know, Mel," he had said, "you can call on the wives for more than just an emergency. They can be your friends to go shopping with or out to lunch with too. All of you are in the same boat here, waiting for your men to come home."

He didn't understand. Those numbers represented pain; those ladies only showed up to help keep a spouse together when there was a major problem—like one of the soldiers getting shot or a death in the family. Calling the team leader's wife meant something was horribly wrong.

And she was about to pick up that phone and admit the

fact that something was horribly wrong in her own home to another person. *Can I say the words? Can I admit out loud what the doctors have told me?*

Her hand shook as she dialed. The phone rang twice before a woman answered with the typical hello.

"Is this Lisa?"

"Yes," the wife of her husband's team leader replied.

"This is Melody, David Podell's wife."

"Oh, hi! How are you?"

"I'm sorry to bother you at home."

"It's not a bother. Really. What's up?"

Melody tried to control the tremor in her voice. She couldn't remember what the woman looked like, although she was certain she had been among the wives at the pre-deployment briefing given by the commander at David's work. "It's our baby, Cole. He's been sick."

"Oh, I'm sorry. Do you need some help? Can I come over and take care of him for a bit so you can get some sleep?"

"Uh, no. It's..." Melody's voice broke as the sobs started. The words wouldn't come out. They tumbled around in her brain and mocked her.

"Oh, honey. What's wrong?"

Melody couldn't stop crying long enough to answer. The fear she'd kept under such tight control since this started ran wild through her imagination. Just a week and a half ago, her baby was fine. Eleven days ago, she'd laid him down for a nap like all the days before. *How'd we get here?* She sunk down on the kitchen floor.

"Melody, I'm on my way. We live just about ten minutes from you. I'll be right there."

MELODY HEARD A SOFT KNOCK, AND THE FRONT DOOR OPENED. "Melody?"

She lifted her head, numb. "I'm here."

Lisa, a curly redhead in trim jeans and cowboy boots, came around the corner. "Hey." She walked over and crouched down near Melody. "What's going on?"

Melody twisted the kitchen towel in her hands. "Cole's in the hospital."

"At Womack or Cape Fear?"

"They just moved him this morning to Duke."

"Duke? Melody, what happened?"

Melody sighed deeply. "It started with RSV. His doctor put him in the hospital when they found out he had pneumonia. As they watched him for that, they found something wrong with his heart."

"How long has he been in the hospital?"

Melody tried to think clearly. "This is Monday?"

Lisa nodded.

"This is day five."

"Oh, girl. Why didn't you call me sooner? You don't need to deal with all this by yourself."

The tears started welling up. Melody looked at Lisa, needing her to understand. "I didn't want to be a bother. I know you are busy, and a lot of ladies are having problems." Melody untwisted the hand towel, focusing for a moment on the weave of the cloth. "It was just a cold."

Lisa sat on the floor beside Melody, putting her hand on her thigh. "So what are the doctors saying now?"

Melody took a deep breath. "His heart problem is called ASD – Atrial something Defect." She tried to recall the terms used. *Atrial Sep...Sepgum? Sep...something.* "I can't remember what the S stands for."

"How bad is it?"

Melody tried to speak but couldn't get the words out. She just shook her head as the tears flowed.

"Take your time, honey."

She gulped. "It's basically a hole in his heart. Some of the blood that's already been to the lungs is able to circle through the heart and go back into the lungs instead of going out to the rest of the body. So his heart is having to work extra hard to pump blood through the body, and his lungs are getting too much blood."

"Are they talking about surgery? Is it something they can fix?"

"They said surgery can be an option, and they are going to evaluate him for a catheterization of some sort—going in through his leg to put something in the heart to block the hole. But they are worried about him surviving any procedure because the pneumonia is so bad."

"Does your husband know any of this?"

Melody shook her head. "He tried to call last week, but we were at the hospital and I missed it. I don't think he's called since."

Lisa confirmed Melody's suspicions. "The guys have been out for several days. All of us are getting anxious to talk to them. Hopefully, they can call home soon."

Melody sat quiet, unsure what to say. She needed so much more than just to talk to David and know he was still alive and unhurt.

"David's bosses at Command don't know anything about this yet?"

"No. I didn't know who to call, and I didn't want David to worry if Cole was just going to fight the pneumonia and be fine again."

"Melody, I think it's time we get them involved. They will want to know this is going on, and David should be updated."

Melody nodded her head and tried to keep a fresh onslaught of tears at bay. "What do I need to do?"

"We'll start by calling the chaplain."

THE NEXT 24 HOURS WERE A BIT OF A WHIRLWIND AS MELODY got caught up in the system. The chaplain called the commander, and then the Red Cross got involved. Word was being sent to David, and they were getting him home on the first thing that moved. The chaplain warned her that it could still take up to a week considering David's location but that he would get priority seating at every stop.

Lisa called two other ladies, and they organized around-the-clock care for Melody. They would man the phones, clean Cole's room from top to bottom, and prepare some easy snacks for her to take with her to the hospital.

Life's getting better, right? Melody stared at the long road to Durham, North Carolina. As she traveled to see Cole, the tall pine trees mocked her wishful thinking. They reminded her of people standing silent, allowing room for pallbearers to accomplish their task.

MELODY STEPPED OUTSIDE THE HOSPITAL ON WEDNESDAY afternoon to get some fresh air. She walked down the sidewalk to a bench and decided to sit for a while where the air didn't smell of disinfectant and the people weren't talking about children getting to go home. Her Cole was not improving.

Her phone vibrated, and she thought about ignoring it so she could soak in a little more peace. *It might be Lisa or the chaplain.* "Hello?"

"Mel!"

"David!"

"How's Cole? What have the doctors said?"

She took a deep breath and closed her eyes as she unloaded the truth of the situation on her husband. "It's not good. They don't think his body could survive the procedure his heart needs right now, but they are asking me if I want them to try. David, I don't know what to do!" Tears started falling gently.

"I'm coming home, Mel. It will probably take another three or four days, but I'm on the next plane."

"Really?"

"Do you have anyone with you? Is anyone helping you through this?"

"The wives of your team mates have been great. They've gone through Cole's room and sanitized it, they made me supper last night, and they are bringing something again tonight. And the chaplain made arrangements to get Mom and Aunt Patricia from the airport to our house later tonight."

"They're both coming in?"

"Yeah." Melody smiled just a bit. "And apparently Aunt Patricia gave Ryan quite the time of it Monday for not telling her everything he knew."

"Ryan?"

"Yeah, I called Brittney last week. I just needed to hear the voice of someone familiar."

"I'm sorry you've had to do this alone, Mel."

"Just come home, David. We need you."

CHAPTER 9

*M*ELODY'S MOM, DOROTHY, TRAVELED to the hospital with her on Thursday. The cardiac catheterization lab, with Melody's permission, scheduled Cole for the procedure to try to position an implant to cover the hole in Cole's heart.

"Did I do the right thing, Mom?" Melody asked as they sat in the waiting room.

Dorothy fixed her gray eyes on her daughter. "You have to try, sweetheart. You heard the doctor say he isn't going to get better until his heart is fixed."

"But what if waiting a couple of days would be better?"

Her mother put the crocheted square she was working on down in her lap and looked at her. "Has the pneumonia been getting any better?"

Melody took a deep breath. "No."

"I know you are looking for certainty, for definite answers." Dorothy shook her head, her short gray and white hair not moving with the motion. "But life doesn't work that way. You have to make the best decisions you can with the information available to you at the time."

"But what if I don't like the results?"

"Melody, you have to stop living in your what-if world. What if a bomb explodes underneath your feet? What if the electricity goes out? What if the surgeon has a heart attack?"

Melody stood and paced away from her mom. *She's right. But this isn't her child. This isn't her decision. The weight of this is on me! What if another day or two would make a difference?*

Glancing at the clock, she continued pacing the waiting room. The doctors had told her the procedure would take about 30 minutes. Much less than that, she'd been warned, and it probably meant they had to quit before it was done. They'd taken him back about 45 minutes ago, after the nurse told her it would take about 30 minutes to prepare him before the doctors could start. *Come on, Cole. You can do this!*

"Honey, come sit down."

"Mom, I can't sit right now. I need to move."

"Moving is not going to help Cole."

"Not moving won't help him either."

She heard her mom sigh. "True."

"Mrs. Podell?"

Melody heard her name called, and her gaze flew to the clock. Fifty minutes. *Oh, no!*

"Yes? I'm Melody Podell."

"Hi. I'm a doctor with the team working on Cole."

Melody approached this new doctor, focusing on his bushy eyebrows to keep her knees from buckling. She felt her mom walk up beside her.

"We were able to get the tube into Cole's leg, but just before we got up to his heart, he took a turn downhill. We had to pull the tube back out and stabilize him."

"So you weren't able to put the patch on?" said Dorothy, the wrinkles on her brow increasing with her expression.

"No, ma'am. We'll give him 24 to 48 hours to recover and see how he's doing."

Melody could barely breathe. *They were almost to his heart and had to stop. Couldn't they push it just a little farther? Didn't they say it was better if his heart was fixed?*

She turned and walked away from the doctor, blindly stopping in front of the chair where her mom had just been sitting. She could hear the doctor and her mom continuing to talk. She probably should listen to their discussion.

But would it make a difference? Why couldn't they just have finished the procedure?

MELODY WALKED INTO COLE'S ISOLATION ROOM WITH TWO cups of coffee the next morning. Aunt Patricia had Doctor K. cornered. Melody almost felt sorry for him, but then she couldn't even remember his full name other than it was something Greek-sounding. *Who is in worse shape right now? Him or me?*

"Now, doc, I'm a bit confused. Why is his heart too big if it's pumping his blood lik'n it's supposed to?"

"Part of his heart is doing an excellent job of pumping the blood, Mrs. Guire. The problem is that since some of the blood is escaping through the hole and recirculating back to the lungs, not all the blood is going to the rest of his body. The heart is having to work extra hard to get the normal blood flow plus the additional blood flow into his lungs."

This doc talks a lot with his hands, Melody noticed. *I wonder if his hands always have to be busy like a mother's hands do.*

"Which is why his heart rate is up?"

"Yes. The heart is basically just a muscle, and when you work out a muscle..." said the doctor.

"It gets bigger." Patricia took the coffee offered by Melody and took a sip.

Melody watched Patricia's hair bounced slightly with

each movement of her head, a stark contrast to her mom's perfectly combed style.

"Mrs. Podell, we're going to run a couple more tests today on your son. I want to check his blood work and also get a fresh echocardiogram."

"Echo?" said Melody. "That's a picture of the heart, right?"

"Sort of. It's an ultrasound."

"What will that do for you, doc?" said Patricia.

"It will give us an update on the pneumonia and how his heart is doing. I'm hearing some new sounds in there, and I want a better idea of what's happening."

"New sounds?" Melody put her hand to her chest. *Could this finally be good news?*

"Yes. It could be a lot of things at this point, so I don't want to get your hopes up."

"You saying the sounds ain't good ones?"

Melody wanted to lash out at her aunt. *Of course the sounds are good ones. This is it! Finally, my baby is fighting and winning!*

"Ma'am, I really can't say until we get the test results. Right now, we can hope for the best because he seems to be stable. I'll have more news for you once I get those test results back."

Melody felt like floating as the doctor left. She turned and looked at her baby. *I knew you could do this, Cole. I knew it!*

MELODY TURNED SHARPLY AWAY FROM THE WINDOW SEVERAL hours later when the alarm sounded. She looked first at her son, then at the machines connected to him. Eyes wide, she looked at the screens, hoping one would hold up a sign to tell her the problem.

A nurse came in, took a brief look at the screens, and

pushed a button. "Well, well, baby boy. Whatcha think you're doing now? We can't be having this, you know?"

"Wh—What's wrong? What happened?"

"He's just not getting quite enough oxygen," said the nurse.

"What's that mean? He ain't breathing?"

Leave it to Aunt Patricia to get straight to the point. *Of course Cole was breathing.* Her eyes flew to Cole's chest. *Wasn't he?*

"Oh, he's breathing, sure enough. He's just not getting enough of the oxygen to his body. His poor lungs are so eat up with the RSV." The nurse watched the monitors for another moment.

"So what are you planning on doing, then?" said Patricia.

"I'll report this to the doctor, but we'll just be giving him a little help for a bit. I'm sure we'll just get him on a nasal cannula so we can get a higher oxygen level down his little nose like it's supposed to. Be back in just a minute!"

The nurse breezed out of the room, leaving Melody at a loss. *But, Cole. You were doing better.*

Part of her wanted to argue against herself. *It's just oxygen.* But it sounded so empty. Hollow. *It feels like a step backwards. Oh, baby.*

"Mrs. Podell. I'm glad I caught you before you left for tonight."

Melody looked at the doctor she'd spoken with earlier in the day. "Do you have the test results back?"

"Yes, and I'm afraid it's not good. The right ventricle of your son's heart is getting smaller."

"Isn't that what we want to happen?" said Patricia.

"No, ma'am," said Dr. K. "His heart wall is now getting

enlarged. His lungs are so consumed with the pneumonia and RSV that he can no longer get enough blood to them to get oxygen."

"What's all that fancy talk mean?" said Patricia. "I don't understand the problem."

"The blood leaves the right side of the heart and goes to the lungs to pick up oxygen. Then it travels back into the left side of the heart and gets pushed out to the rest of the body to provide the organs with oxygen so they can work properly."

"So turn up the oxygen. Your nurse has been in here a couple times today doing that."

"It's not that simple, ma'am. Turning up the oxygen helps, but it doesn't fix the problem, which is the hole in his heart."

"Cole," said Melody.

"Ma'am?" The doctor looked at her as if she'd lost her mind.

"His name is Cole."

The doctor's face softened, filling with pity as he looked at her. "Mrs. Podell, I'm sorry. I know this isn't easy."

"Do you?" Melody looked directly at the doctor, then continued quietly. "Do you really know?"

"So what's your plan now?" said Patricia.

The doctor looked at her and then at Melody. "We're going to keep a careful watch over him all night. Hopefully, something will give. Ideally, we need that RSV to begin to break apart." The doctor looked back at Melody. "If you're a praying woman, that's what I would ask for."

CHAPTER 10

*M*ELODY TOSSED AND TURNED IN bed that night, desperate for sleep. *Thank goodness Mom is here. She's at least got the house in order for David's arrival.*

Her husband had called earlier while she'd been at the hospital with Aunt Patricia. He'd be landing in Raleigh, North Carolina, tomorrow night.

Will Cole last that long?

She turned and looked at the clock. *It's 1:17. Maybe something warm to drink will help.*

She opened her door and saw a faint glow coming from the living room. Padding down the hallway, she peeked into the living room and saw Aunt Patty. Her eyes were closed, but her lips were moving and her Bible sat in her lap. Melody just shook her head and turned to the kitchen.

She stared into her open refrigerator, but nothing looked appealing. Finally grabbing the milk, she turned to get a mug. Aunt Patty stood in the doorway. "I didn't expect you to be awake."

"Just seeking a bit of wisdom from God," said Patricia.

"Did He bother to give you any?"

"Yes."

Melody wanted to slam her cup down and scream *He's a fraud!* She squeezed her eyes closed and rubbed her temple. "Well, ain't that special."

"Melody, do you know that it's okay to be mad at God?"

"What?" Melody couldn't believe she was having this conversation.

"He isn't scared that you might throw a temper tantrum. In fact, He'd prefer that to what you're currently doing."

Melody took a deep breath and clenched her fists. "God does not care about me, and He clearly does not care about Cole."

"You're wrong."

"Patricia!" Melody's mom stood across the living room, witnessing the exchange through the open breakfast bar lining one kitchen wall. "What are you doing?"

Patricia turned to face her sister. "We can't keep tiptoeing around her. She's in a wrestling match with the Almighty, and all she wants to do is sit in a corner and pout!"

"I don't quite see how telling her to throw a temper tantrum is helpful. Her child is fighting for his life!"

"Is he?" Patricia asked pointedly.

"Is he what?"

"Is he fighting for his life?"

Melody gasped and clung to the counter for support. Her mom stormed closer to Patricia.

"What are you saying?"

"I'm just wondering if maybe that child has a better grasp of the eternal than we do. Maybe he's not fighting for himself. Maybe he's fighting for his momma's soul."

Dorothy threw her hands up in the air. "I don't even know how to respond to that!"

"Then quit talking and do some listening for once. This world is not all about us. But God will use this world to draw us closer to Him." Patricia aimed her finger at Dorothy's face. "Your child is turning her back on Him. She's angry and won't near admit it. I know you see it. But you won't address it."

"She has a right to be angry!"

"Of course she does! But holdin' it all in ain't doin' none of us any good. She's..."

"Enough!" Melody put her hands up to her ears. "Enough. Quit talking about me like I'm not in the room. Just..." Melody shook her head. "Just quit talking!"

She pushed through the two women and stormed to her bedroom, slamming the door behind her. *How dare they! How dare she! Aunt Patty started all this. If she'd ever had any children, she would know better. She would know that I only have Cole's best interests at heart. I'm making the best decisions I can for my son so he can live.*

A sob escaped her. She fell onto her bed and cried into her pillow. Eventually, she fell asleep.

MELODY STOOD AT THE TOP OF A HILL WATCHING THREE children play in the field below. A woman ran with them, twirling and laughing. Melody longed to join them but held back.

The woman turned and looked at her. She beckoned, yet Melody couldn't force her legs to move forward to join in the fun.

She looked behind her and saw Cole nestled in the arms of a man she didn't know; his focus was completely on her child. Uncertain, she called to the man, and he looked at her. His blue eyes seemed to pierce her heart, and she gasped.

"Who are you?"

The man quietly looked at her, then toward the sky. He began to float, rising from the earth.

"Wait!"

Her words had no affect on him.

She raced toward him. "My baby! Give me back my baby!"

An alarm burst through her senses, and Melody covered her ears with both hands, cowering near the ground.

Suddenly she turned, flinging bed covers and sitting upright. "My baby!"

Disoriented, she looked around the dark room. *A dream. It was just a dream.* She ran her fingers through her hair and tried to calm down.

Her mom knocked before opening the door. "Melody, honey?"

She sighed. "Yeah, Mom?"

"The hospital is on the phone. They say it's urgent."

The alarm. The phone. My baby! Melody scrambled over to David's side of the bed and grabbed the phone.

"Hello? This is Melody Podell."

"Mrs. Podell. I'm Dr. Campbell, one of the doctors working on your son. Throughout the night, his oxygen saturation has continued to drop. We tried increasing the flow through his nasal cannula, but it wasn't enough. His O2 sats dropped into the 50s, so we've had to intubate him and put him on a ventilator."

"Intubate?" Melody could hardly breathe herself.

"Yes, ma'am. We put a tube down his throat and connected it to a machine to help him breathe."

"So he's okay now?"

"Well, the machine wasn't helping enough, so we also started him on inhaled nitric oxide. Ideally, this opens up the lungs's blood vessels to allow more blood flow."

"Ideally?"

"Your son's lungs are so full of mucus from the RSV, the nitric oxide just isn't working."

Melody rubbed her temple. "What does that mean?"

"We've started several PICC lines—"

"PICC lines?"

"IV lines into his arms so we can give him more medicine. We've added dopamine and dobutamine to increase his blood pressure and an epinephrine drip to strengthen his heart's ability to contract. We've also sedated and paralyzed him."

"Was that necessary?"

"Ma'am, we're doing everything we can, but the last thing we need is for him to fight against those tubes."

"Okay. That makes sense, I guess."

"Mrs. Podell, considering everything he's been through tonight, you need to know that things do not look good. Quite honestly, I don't know how long his body is going to hold out."

Melody felt the tears gathering.

"I need to ask you if you want us to continue all possible life-saving measures until his body gives out, or if you'd prefer to sign a Do Not Resuscitate order."

Melody's hand flew to her mouth as she listened to the doctor.

"We've given him everything there is to give him. He needs surgery to have a fair chance, but he's too sick to survive the procedure. His O2 sats are currently in the low 80s, and his heart rate is in the 190s. He's in critical condition."

She took a deep breath. "What exactly does a Do Not Resuscitate order mean?"

"We won't stop any of his medications, and we'll continue to help him fight the RSV as best we can. But if his heart gives out, we won't do CPR or use any life-saving medications."

"I...I just don't know. Can I think about it?"

"Of course. The nurses have the paperwork if you decide you want to sign it."

Melody could barely function as the doctor hung up. Tears streamed down her face as the hand holding the phone dropped to her lap.

"Oh, honey." Melody's mom took the phone and sat down beside her. She felt her hair being stroked.

"I want my baby, Mom." She turned into her mom's open arms and buried her face into her mom's shoulder as the sobs came. "I want my baby."

CHAPTER 11

*A*FRAID OF WHAT SHE MIGHT FIND, **Melody** had taken her time getting to the hospital the next morning. Now that she was looking at her son through the window, she couldn't make herself go in. Cole didn't look alive.

Outside of the ventilator's steady pumping of his chest, she saw no movement. Tubes or wires seemed to be coming from every part of his body, connected to machines that had multiplied overnight. And his color was a sickening shade of gray.

"Come on, honey."

Her mom's hand on her shoulder offered little comfort as she forced herself through the doorway. "Maybe I shouldn't have come."

"Melody. You need to be here. You'd..."

"Need? I *need* to be here, Mom?" Melody felt her throat tightening and her eyes burning. "To do what? Please tell me exactly what I'm supposed to do!"

"Ma'am?" A nurse in blue scrubs popped through the doorway. "I can only imagine how difficult this must be, but I'm going to have to ask you to hold it down or step outside.

I can't have you yelling in here and disturbing any of the babies." She looked at Cole and back at Melody. "Including your own."

Melody closed her eyes and took a deep breath. "Sorry." She refocused on the nurse before her. "I'll try to be more quiet."

"All right. Is there anything I can get you? Answer any questions?"

Melody looked at her son, her Cole. Fresh tears coated her eyes and overflowed. She could barely squeak out a response to the kind nurse waiting so patiently. "His daddy will be home tonight from Afghanistan. Will he make it until then?"

"Your baby's holding steady right now. There are a couple things we can do to help him hold on. Have you signed the DNR?"

Melody shook her head. "I don't know if I can. I don't want to give up on him. What if he just needs a little more time?" Melody looked at the nurse. "Couldn't the medicine still work? Haven't other babies survived when the doctors thought there was no hope?"

Melody appreciated the look she saw in the nurse's eyes. She saw kindness, not pity. Sadness. *This nurse really cares.*

"I'll tell you, ma'am. I've worked in the PICU for almost 20 years, and I've seen a lot of amazing things that the doctors couldn't explain. But I also know a lot about the body and how it works. I believe God could step in and heal your son, and some of the doctors here would be absolutely baffled."

The nurse looked at the monitors that filled her brief pause with beeps as they worked. "But without that miracle, these machines tell me your baby is hurting. We've made him comfortable, and he may not consciously know he's in pain, but honey, his body is shutting down on him.

Whether you sign the DNR or not, he doesn't have a lot of time left."

"So, why should I sign it, then? If it's not going to make a difference?"

"There are certainly some things we can do if his little heart stops beating to try to get it going again. We can perform CPR and give him some medications. But most likely, with him in the condition he's in, all it's going to do is prolong the inevitable, probably do him more harm than good, and send you on a roller coaster of emotions."

Melody looked at Cole. *Signing that paper means giving up, but what hope do I have?* "If it's possible, I'd like him to make it until his daddy gets here."

MELODY SAT IN THE CHAIR BY COLE'S BED, HER FACE TURNED to the door. People walked by, but she couldn't really focus on any of it. It felt like her life was one drawn out day after another. Part of her longed to escape. Part of her waited for the next bit of bad news. The news was always bad.

"Melody, honey, why don't we go for a walk?"

Her mother had been flitting about the room for the last ten minutes, straightening up as if they were just visiting a friend and needed to clean up behind themselves.

"I don't want to go for a walk, Mom."

"It's a beautiful, sunny day."

Melody didn't respond.

"It's a lovely October day out there. A little sun would do us good."

Melody closed her eyes. "I don't want to."

"Come on. We could walk a couple blocks and find a nice place to get some lunch."

Melody rubbed her temples. "We're not on vacation,

Mom. Warm sunshine and a nice lunch are not going to change what is happening in this room. My baby is still dying."

"Yes, he is. But you still need to eat."

"I don't think I can."

"Come on. My treat."

Dorothy grabbed her purse and walked to the door, pausing long enough to give Melody the impression that this wasn't negotiable. Truth was, Melody didn't have the strength to fight her.

They walked out the front doors of the hospital and turned left. Melody simply kept pace with her mom as they walked.

Near the corner of Research Drive, Melody caught the eyes of a woman walking towards them. The woman smiled, and Melody returned the gesture as best she could.

Just as they were about to pass each other, the woman spoke. "God loves you."

Melody came to an abrupt stop and looked at her. "What?"

"Whatever is going on in your life, God loves you."

Melody sucked in her breath. "Why would you say that to a stranger on the street?"

Melody's mom reached out and touched her arm.

The woman shrugged. "Something told me that you needed the reminder." She took a couple steps and looked over her shoulder. "Look for Him. He's waiting."

"Him? Who?" *What is she talking about?*

The woman simply looked up before looking back at Melody. Then, after an understanding smile, she continued on her way.

Melody stood dumbfounded for a moment. *God? She wants me to look for God? Who does she think she is?*

"Melody?"

She turned and looked at her mom. "Who does she think she is?"

"Come on." Her mom began to walk towards Erwin Terrace, and Melody followed.

"You can't just go around telling people stuff like that. She has no right!"

Melody's mother gave a slight sigh. "She has the right to speak if she wants to."

"She has no idea what I'm going through. How dare she infer God cares! That He's waiting. Waiting for what? Cole to die? This is not love! This is not what love looks like!"

Her mom spun around. "Maybe He's waiting on you to stop having this constant temper tantrum!"

Melody gasped. "My child is dying!"

"And he's my grandchild and Patricia's nephew. His illness affects more than you. We've put our lives on hold to fly out here to help."

"Then go home."

"That's *not* the point! Cole is important to us. But when is the last time you got out of your own head long enough to find out how I was doing, how I'm holding up?"

"It's not about you!"

Dorothy stopped and inhaled deeply. "You're right, Melody. It's not about me. Cole's illness, David's deployment, you moving across the country from all your family and friends—none of it is about me."

She pointed her finger at Melody. "But it's not about you, either."

Melody looked at her briefly. She couldn't believe they were having this conversation, let alone on a busy street just down from the hospital. She clenched her fists and tried to control her breathing. "I'm going back to Cole's room. Enjoy your lunch."

MELODY GLANCED AT THE CLOCK FOR THE MILLIONTH TIME AS she sat in the chair by Cole's bed. It was 8:17. She waited for David. One of the chaplains from Ft. Bragg was picking him up at the airport and bringing him straight to the hospital.

Her mother had left just before 6:00pm, driving Melody's Accord home. Not that they had really spoken since their argument on the street. She said she wanted to spend a quiet evening with her sister. Melody doubted that Aunt Patricia was going to be quiet. The woman had gotten increasingly vocal about God's plan in all this, and she could only imagine what would be said about the afternoon spat.

A tear fell down Melody's cheek, and she looked at what was once her lively baby. *God, if You really are out there, I don't like Your plan.*

CHAPTER 12

HE PLANE TOUCHED DOWN, AND David had to force himself to remain seated. He had left Kunar Province Wednesday afternoon, which was early Wednesday morning in North Carolina. Now it was Saturday.

"Ladies and gentlemen," said the flight attendant, "we know you have a choice when flying, and we'd like to thank you for flying with us today. The pilot will have us at the gate in just a moment and will turn off the seatbelt sign when it is safe for you to get up from your seats. Local time is 7:26pm.

"If I may have your attention for just another moment, tonight we have a soldier traveling with us, home from Afghanistan and trying to get to Duke University Children's Hospital to see his son. I respectfully ask that everyone remain seated and allow him to leave the plane first."

David teared up at the flight attendant's gesture. In the last four days, he'd traveled 9,000 miles, and he had seen God's hand several times. Teammates prayed him safely out of Kunar, a helicopter pilot who happened to be heading in the right direction, a kind nurse who had been seated beside him on the flight out of Frankfurt, Germany, and sweet

USO volunteers who had provided shaving cream, razors, and soap during his layover in Chicago. Thank goodness he'd had to time to wash up and change into a fresh uniform.

The seatbelt sign released, and David bolted out of his seat, popped the overhead compartment, and grabbed his bag. Just before leaving the plane, he stopped to look back at his fellow air travelers. Struggling to hold back the tears, he simply nodded his head. "Thank you."

A chaplain was waiting for him, and they headed for the parking garage.

"Do you know anything, sir?"

"Not much, Sergeant. But I understand time is critical."

David set his jaw as he followed the man to the government-issued vehicle. *Father, let me make it in time.*

DAVID STOOD SPEECHLESS IN THE DOORWAY OF HIS SON'S hospital room. His heart froze at the stillness of his child, lying there barely recognizable. *My boy has been replaced by a swollen, discolored...*

No kind word came to mind.

Sitting in the chair near the crib, Melody turned and saw him standing there. "David!" She sprang up and into his arms, sobbing.

Instinctively, he wrapped his arms around her and held her tight. *God, You've got this, right?*

Releasing Melody, he moved closer to the crib, taking in all the machines. He cleared his throat, hoping his voice would cooperate. "What are the doctors saying?"

"There's nothing more they can do. He needs surgery to have a chance, but the RSV and pneumonia have taken over his lungs, and he's too weak. They've got him on pain meds now—and a ventilator. And they've sedated him and paralyzed him so he won't fight the tubes."

"So there's no hope?" David couldn't believe he was saying that. He looked at her, hoping to see something in her eyes that would tell him he was overreacting.

She just shook her head and wiped at the tears.

"I want to hold him."

"David, you can't. Not with everything connected to him."

"He's not dying alone in that bed."

"We're right here! I've been right beside him all day!"

"Mel, I need to hold him. I left him, maybe when he needed me most. I won't abandon him now."

"Is there a problem in here?" A heavyset nurse pushed past the chaplain, who was still standing in the doorway.

David turned to face the nurse standing like a formidable tank before him. "I want to hold my son."

"David, you can't."

"Let me go get a doctor." The nurse strode out of the room, and Melody turned away from David. Neither spoke as they waited. Minutes ticked past, and David struggled to control his urge to grab Cole.

"Evening, folks. I'm Dr. Campbell, the doctor on duty this evening. Can I answer any questions for you?"

David automatically sized up the doctor as he'd been trained to size up the Afghan villagers, looking for people friendly to the American forces. About David's height and weight, he seemed professional and a straight shooter. "I want to hold my son," said David.

"Okay. Have you been updated on his condition?"

"Needs heart surgery, won't survive it, sick with RSV and pneumonia." David heard Melody's gasp and realized how cold his synopsis must sound. "Look doctor, I left North Carolina with a healthy baby boy. Down range, I'm told he's dying. Is that accurate?"

The doctor sighed. "Yes, it is."

"Are these machines keeping him alive?"

"Not entirely. But they are greatly assisting. He probably would not last long without the ventilator."

"And how long does he have if we leave him as he is now?"

The doctor looked at David for a moment before answering. "A few days. Probably less."

Melody looked ready to crumble into a heap on the floor. David slipped an arm around her shoulders.

"So, what needs to happen for me to be able to hold him?"

"I need to get a little more information from you; then we'll get you situated. Are you looking to hold him while he's still connected to everything, or do you want us to pull him off the ventilator?"

"Doesn't he need the ventilator to breathe?"

"Yes, as long as the paralytic is in his system."

"I don't fully understand. How can the ventilator be an option?"

"We can cut off the paralytic," the doctor explained, "and it would slowly work itself out of his system. Once he began to regain some movement, we could remove the tubes and get him off it."

"What does all that mean for his life expectancy?" David felt Melody leaning more heavily against him.

"If we take the ventilator out now, he'd only last about ten minutes. The muscles just wouldn't regain movement fast enough, and his body would be deprived of oxygen. If we cut the paralytic now, he would need to remain on the ventilator for about two hours. Then he should have sufficient control to breathe on his own for a short time."

"How short?"

"It's hard to say..."

"Doctor, how long?"

The doctor glanced from Melody to David. "Thirty minutes. Maybe an hour. I don't think his heart can take much more than that."

David squeezed Melody tight. "Make it happen."

"No!" Melody struggled out of David's embrace. "David, you can't give up on him."

"Mel, it doesn't matter if we cut the paralytic and pull the ventilator or not. Cole's not going to get a different outcome. But we can hold him close in his final moments."

Melody walked over to the chair and sat down hard.

"I need to do this, Mel. I need to hold my son."

She stared at the crib for a moment. "I don't think I can."

He crouched before her, grabbing her hands. "I'll do it for both of us."

David watched the tears stream down her face and a flood of emotions pass through her eyes. Finally, she nodded.

FOR TWO HOURS DAVID PATIENTLY HELD COLE, CAREFULLY maneuvering around tubes and wires until he began to see the boy's eyes flutter. The nurses had come in then to disconnect him from the ventilator, and now David held him close and stroked the peach fuzz on his head. His son moved occasionally, and David could almost pretend the child was just sleeping instead of sedated.

David hummed softly. He tried to take in every part of his child, purposely bringing memories to the front of his mind. Watching his birth had been the highlight of his twenty-two years. Until Cole smiled. *Nothing is as great as your smile, boy.*

He'd looked forward to Cole's first steps and teaching him to ride a bike. Now he'd have to reconcile missing most of his child's short life. *Duty called and I answered, but I missed so much of you.*

David let the tears flow as he looked at Cole's tiny fingers. Fingers that never got to build with blocks or throw a football. *Oh, God, how do I survive this? How am I supposed to go on from here?*

Just as he thought his emotions would get the best of him, Melody returned from calling her mom. Unshed tears and unspoken questions filled her eyes, questions she didn't seem to want to voice. Questions he probably didn't have answers to, anyway.

He shifted Cole to one arm and opened his other to his wife. She gently sat in his lap, wrapping one arm around his neck and the other around their son.

Barely above a whisper, David heard Melody say, "I love you, Cole."

"We both love you, son," said David. "We'll never forget you."

CHAPTER 13

*D*AVID WOKE THE NEXT MORNING, unwilling to move. Exhaustion from the physical and emotional turmoil of the last several days felt like it had settled deep in his bones. His body felt like he could sleep another three days. But his mind only saw Cole lying in that hospital bed, and his heart only felt the depression of walking away from his baby.

Today they had to make funeral choices, including what they wanted to do with him after his cremation. *A burial plot here in North Carolina would be easiest, but how long will the Army keep us stationed here? And when I retire, will we stay? Perhaps buying an urn and keeping him with us would be best. Could I stand to have his remains in the house? God, I need some wisdom.*

He heard Melody stirring beside him, so he rolled over to her. Eyes full of tears, she simply looked at him and said, "I want my baby."

He pulled her close. "I know. Me too."

DAVID STEPPED OUTSIDE AND TOOK A DEEP BREATH. *Sunny day, huh? God, couldn't You put up a few clouds for me?*

The house was largely quiet, even with the small flow of people stopping by to see them. One of the pastors from their church had come, as had a chaplain who had assured him that he would contact the personnel support element so the Casualty Office could get involved. At least Aunt Patricia and Dorothy were being kept occupied with visits from his team's various spouses.

He leaned against the deck railing and dialed a familiar number.

"Hello?"

"Hey, Ryan."

"David! Are you home?"

"Yeah."

"How's Cole?"

David still had trouble saying the words. His eyes still burned from the conversations with his parents and older brother. "He didn't make it."

Silence lingered on the other end of the line. "I'm sorry."

"We opted to donate whatever organs they could use for other children."

"I know those families appreciate your sacrifice."

"This is one I'd have rather not made."

"I can imagine."

"I never think about it being a sacrifice when I'm in survival training or have to leave Mel behind to deploy somewhere. It's my job, and I'm good at it. I know the Army is what I'm supposed to do."

"But this is different?"

"I don't see the purpose, Ryan. Why did God choose this, or allow this, or whatever you want to call it?"

"I don't know, David."

"I understand war. I know we need a military force to

stand up to evil men. I know sometimes soldiers get hurt or die, and it may seem random, but that's part of the package deal. I get that. I walk into it knowing it could be me. But Cole didn't get a choice. He didn't get a vote in whether or not to sacrifice himself for the good of others."

"I wish I had answers for you. All I know is that God is trustworthy, even when He doesn't make sense."

"Maybe that's why I'm looking for a purpose. I believe I can trust Him, but... I don't know. Maybe my heart is just trying to catch up with my head."

"I can understand that."

David looked at his back shed and noticed a bird sitting on top of the roof. *How many worries do birds have?*

"What can I do, Dave? You want me to fly out there?"

"My commander's given me some time off, and I've got some leave to burn. I think we're going to inter him in Sacramento near our parents and then head north to see you and Brittany for a few days, if that's okay. Melody needs the time away, and I think the time with Britt will be good for her."

"Before you come, you need to know something." Ryan paused. "Amber and Brittany are both pregnant."

David took a deep breath and blew it out. "Wow. I wish I could be more happy for you."

"It's okay. And I understand if you don't come."

David paused. "No, I still think we should. Every time I ask God for help to get through this, you come to mind. I think we need to be in Crossing for a bit."

"Okay. We'll be waiting."

DAVID WORRIED. ALTHOUGH SIMPLE, THE INTERMENT ceremony had been nice, and Melody had held it together fairly well—until it was time to walk away. He had to admit walking away from the columbarium had been the toughest thing he'd ever done.

Now, with his son safely tucked into his niche, they were heading north on I-5. Melody sulked in the passenger seat beside him.

"Want some lunch?"

"Not really."

"Might do you some good."

"I'm not hungry."

"It's still a long way to Crossing."

"Then let's turn around and go back to Mom's."

"And what are you going to do there? Mope? Sit in your room?"

She glared at him. "So what if I do? Don't I have the right to mope? I just buried my baby!"

"But what about those of us who are still living? I need you too, Mel."

She snorted. "Right. I'm so necessary to your well-being that you spend more time in the field or deployed than you do at home."

David gripped the steering wheel harder. "Don't you want to see Brittany?"

"Why? So she can rub her pregnancy in my face?"

"She wouldn't do that!"

"She's a fool, anyway."

"What do you mean by that?"

"She's probably living in some dreamland, thinking she'll give birth to a beautiful baby and they'll live happily ever after."

"That's the real problem."

"What?"

"You're angry because she still has her baby."

"I just don't live in a fantasy anymore."

"We won't feel like this forever, Mel. Our hearts will heal; we'll be able to have another baby."

"No."

"No, what?"

"No more babies. I won't be hurt like this again."

CHAPTER 14

*M*ELODY SUNK LOWER IN THE front seat of her mom's 2011 Ford Taurus as David pulled off Highway 26 and entered Crossing. *I can't believe Mom loaned David the car for this stupid trip. What's wrong with sitting in Sacramento, seeing all our friends there?*

"Which road does your Aunt Patricia live on?"

"Hood."

"Will you recognize the house?"

"It shouldn't be too hard. This whole town's only about twelve blocks."

David turned right onto Hood Street and drove slowly.

Melody pointed ahead and to the left. "There. The bright blue one."

"She does have an eccentric flair, doesn't she?"

Melody looked at the ranch-style home with blue siding as David parked. The stone path led to wide steps and a broad front porch complete with white corner block crowns. Even the top peak of the house boasted gable decorations. Certainly not the kind of thing people put money into anymore.

"Ready?"

Melody took a deep breath. "I guess."

David squeezed her hand and got out. Melody saw her aunt standing on the top step but couldn't quite make out what she was saying. She closed her eyes. *I hope David was right about coming here.*

Her door opened, and the conversation drifted to her ears.

"The trip up was pretty uneventful. The scenery was beautiful. It's been a long time since I've driven Interstate 5 out of California."

Sounds harmless enough. Melody stepped out and plastered on her best smile.

On the front porch, her aunt gave her a hug before leading the way into the small living room packed with her collection of trinkets and pictures.

"Do you want anything to eat?"

"No, thanks," said Melody.

"We ate dinner a couple of hours ago," said David.

"Well, come on in. Sit down." Patricia took the floral-patterned chair, leaving the plush blue couch to David and Melody. David scooted a couple of pillows aside to allow more room.

"I'm so glad you came," said Patricia. "I believe God has something special for you here."

Melody bit her tongue.

Her aunt continued. "I don't quite know what He's thinking, of course, but I just feel it in my bones."

"You have some new things since I was last here," said Melody, trying to change the subject.

Patricia looked around. "Yes, well. I just can't pass up a good deal." Her eyes sparkled. "And times lately have been hard for folks. But God keeps providing."

"That curio cabinet is beautiful," said Melody. She walked over to it, doing her best to admire the items it held.

"Yes, that's from a woman about a year or so ago. Her husband had died, and she was cleaning out her house, getting rid of most of her furniture so she could move in with her daughter."

"So she gave that to you?" said David.

"Oh, no. We traded. She needed new tires for her car."

Melody watched the look of confusion on David's face. "Aunt Patricia owns a couple of garages, one here in Crossing and another in Portland. When people can't pay in cash, she trades for whatever they do have."

"I host some of the best estate and yard sales in the county," said Patricia, winking at David.

"You're an amazing woman," said David.

"Just doing my best to work with what God gave me," said Patricia.

Melody sighed. *Does every topic have to lead back to God?*

"So, how is the garage doing?" said Melody.

"Both are doing just fine. Business is a little slower than I'd like, but we're still making enough money to pay the bills."

"How do you manage a shop in Portland?" said David. "Do you run up there regularly?"

"Oh goodness, no. Several years ago, I took on a partner named Jake. He's been such a blessing. Honest, hard-working man. He takes care of the day-to-day stuff, and he and I consult once a month or so."

"How do you know he's not robbing you blind?" said Melody sourly.

"I hire an auditor to check over the books once a year. Plus, a couple times a year, I go up and spend the day with Jake's family. We go to church together and then enjoy a nice lunch somewhere."

Melody continued to look at the various items tucked away on shelves and in corners around the room.

"Surely, Melody," said Patricia, "you've seen enough kindness in people over the last couple of weeks to know that a lot of people can still be trusted."

"Just because people go to church doesn't make them trustworthy," said Melody without facing her aunt.

"And just because bad things happen doesn't mean God isn't."

Melody spun on her aunt. "What's that supposed to mean?"

"God is still trustworthy."

Is she kidding me? "And what exactly in the last year and a half would convince me of that?"

"Melody," said David.

"He gave you that precious baby!" said Patricia.

"He took my baby!" said Melody.

"Melody," said David, standing.

Melody looked at him, then turned around to face the wall. She clenched her fists. *I knew this was a bad idea.*

"It's been a long day," said David. "Why don't I get our bags, Mel? Then you can lay down to rest."

Melody couldn't bring herself to speak, and apparently neither could Patricia.

"Which room would you like us to use, Patricia?" said David.

"That first door on the hall will be fine."

"I'll help you get the bags." Melody turned and stormed out the door.

When David reached the trunk, she turned on him. "I knew this was a bad idea. This isn't going to work, David. I can't stay here with her."

"Why?"

"Why what?"

"Why can't you stay here with your own aunt?"

"What kind of question is that? You were there." Melody pointed at the house. "You heard her."

David popped the trunk open. "What I heard is a woman who believes with her whole heart that God is good."

"Exactly! What a crock!"

"Melody! Are you listening to yourself?"

"Yes! She's in there spouting off all this goody-two-shoes nonsense." She grabbed their small backpack filled with her cosmetics and his shaving kit. "I'm just standing up for what I believe."

"You're standing up for what you are seeing through eyes clouded with grief."

"So I'm not allowed to have an opinion now?"

"You shouldn't demean others in the declaration of theirs. You're belittling her opinions simply because you're hurting."

"I have a right to my opinion!"

David grabbed the suitcase out of the trunk and slammed the lid.

"And so does she."

Melody looked at David's back as he strode to the porch. Her mind felt jumbled. *A few weeks ago, I would have cringed at someone who put down another's opinion. Am I being as harsh as he makes it sound?*

"Come inside, Mel."

David waited for her at the top step. She slung the backpack over her shoulder and walked back into the house.

CHAPTER 15

*D*AVID FOLLOWED THE DIRECTIONS Patricia had given him and pulled into Ryan's driveway. The front porch light on the one-story log cabin beckoned to him, calling out like a lighthouse in a safe harbor. As he approached the front door, it opened. The sight of his friend in blue jeans and a casual sweater brought calmness to his heart. Ryan's short brown hair spiked in an unkempt manner reminded David of more carefree days.

"Hey!" Ryan engulfed him in a hug. "I'm glad you came."

David didn't have any words. He just smiled at his friend.

"Come on in."

Brittany stood from her seat on the overstuffed leather couch, reaching to hug David as he greeted her.

"You look great," said David, unzipping his jacket. Marriage hadn't seemed to add much to her trim figure, and her eyes hadn't lost their sparkle. She just exuded a fun-loving personality.

"Thanks," said Brittany.

"How far along are you?" The smallest bump was beginning to show on her abdomen underneath her long-sleeved t-shirt. *But her taller frame would probably carry a baby better than Melody's.* Brittany had a good three inches on his wife.

"Fifteen weeks. Thankfully, the morning sickness is easing up a bit."

David nodded his head. He looked at Ryan. "And how far is your sister?"

"She's at what," said Ryan, looking at Brittany. "Thirty-three weeks?"

Brittany nodded her head. "She's due just a couple weeks before Christmas."

"So, one baby for the holidays and another for the spring," said David. "Sounds like a great way to end one year and start a new one."

"How are you doing?" said Ryan. He sat beside his wife as David took the chair near them.

"I'm not sure I can put it into words. I get this call while I'm in the desert that my son is sick and the Red Cross is getting me home on the first thing that's moving. And I get home just in time to say goodbye to him." David looked at Ryan. "I was barely home half of his life. Between training for the mission and then leaving when he was about three and a half months old, I only got a few weeks with him."

"How's Melody?" Brittany asked, leaning forward, concern etched on her face.

David rubbed his eyes and sighed deeply. "Angry is probably the best word for it. And she feels justified."

"Anger is one of the stages of grief." Brittany nodded knowingly.

"But it feels like she's stuck there. And she doesn't care to move on."

"What do you mean?" said Ryan.

David leaned forward with his elbows on his thighs. "I

think she's angry at God but taking it out on everyone else. She laid into her aunt tonight just because Patricia said God was trustworthy."

"I'm not sure I would handle someone telling me about the goodness of God very well if I'd just lost my baby," Brittany admitted.

"I get that. I guess." David leaned back again. "I just don't know what to do with her. She hated the idea of coming here. And I think she's avoiding seeing you guys just because of your baby."

"What if Ryan met you tomorrow without me?" Brittany looked at Ryan. "Dr. Williams and I could hold down the office easily enough for a few hours while you meet for lunch or something."

"We could meet at the diner in the town square," said Ryan. "Or I could meet you at the house, and we could walk up. It's just a couple of blocks."

"I'm willing to try anything. Losing Cole is tough. I don't want to lose my wife too."

DAVID LISTENED FOR THE RUMBLE OF RYAN'S FORD MUSTANG the next day. The tension in the air was giving him a headache, and he didn't know whether to take his wife's quiet demeanor as an improvement or not. The cloudy day outside certainly wasn't helping.

"Sounds like Ryan coming," said Patricia from her seat on the couch. She barely looked up from her crossword puzzle.

David listened and barely heard the small block 302. "How far away can you hear that?"

"Oh, through most the town, I suppose. If'n I'm listening for it."

David stood and waited by the front door for Ryan to park the car and walk up to the door. "Hey, man," he greeted his friend. "I'll see if Mel is ready to go."

Ryan nodded his head and stepped inside. "Morning, Mrs. Guire. How are you?"

"Can't say I have any direct complaints."

"Any indirect ones I should know about?"

"Now, boy, don't you think if'n I wanted you all up in my business, I'd make an appointment?"

"Aunt Patricia!" Melody gasped.

Ryan ignored her for the moment and spoke directly to Patricia. "No, ma'am."

Patricia looked at him, her eyes squinted. "No, ma'am, what?"

"I don't think you'd make an appointment."

Patricia looked back to her crossword, dismissing him. "Hmph. You're probably right about that. Have a good lunch."

David and Melody grabbed jackets and joined Ryan, walking down the stairs and toward the sidewalk. "Why did you let her talk to you like that?"

Ryan thumbed back at the house. "That? That was nothing."

"Nothing?" said Melody. "She was downright rude!"

David hung quietly behind, letting the two of them walk side-by-side.

"Nah. Different people show love different ways. Even God romances His people differently. Think about the stories of God calling Abraham and Moses. In one instance He shows up in person and allows Abraham to feed Him. In the other, He presents to Moses in a burning bush and demands that Moses remove His shoes."

Melody shook her head. "What does that have to do with Aunt Patty?"

"It's all about relationship, Mel. Patricia likes to be in charge, and she knows I'll let her have it without giving up any control myself." Ryan shrugged. "I don't see it as rude because I know her heart."

"I suppose you're implying that I don't," said Melody, bristling.

"No," said Ryan. "I'm just saying that what you saw is our relationship. On the outside, she's gruff and controlling. On the inside, she loves very deeply. I won her over the first time I let her help me make a decision on a part for the Mustang. She may not sound like it, but she'd fight for me like I was her own if I needed her to do so."

"Maybe," said Melody, unconvinced.

They turned the corner onto Cascade Street. David saw the diner halfway down the block.

Ryan bumped Melody's arm with his elbow. "It's good to see you, by the way."

She looked at him and sighed. "Thanks. I just… I don't know."

"It's okay, Mel. You lost your baby just ten days ago. Give yourself a break."

They found seats in the diner and took time to decide what to eat. As the waitress walked away, a cute, dark-haired beauty slid into the bench seat beside Ryan.

"Hey, Dr. Ryan!"

"Hey, gorgeous!" He wrapped his arm around the bench behind her. "Aren't you supposed to be in school?"

"Yeah, but I had to get shots." She raised her right sleeve to show her bandage. "Daddy let me come back here for lunch."

"Ah. Did Mrs. Brittany remember to give you candy when she was all done?"

"Yeah. But she didn't give me two like you always do."

Ryan chuckled. "Perhaps she needs more training in the fine art of shot giving."

"I think she's just thinking like a momma."

Ryan chuckled. "Maybe so."

"Are these your friends?"

"Yes. Eleni, I would like you to meet Mr. David and Mrs. Melody. Eleni's father is the cook here."

"How old are you?" said David.

"Six. But I've known Ryan since I was four. He fixed my elbow."

Ryan looked at David. "She'd fallen on some ice and dislocated it."

David smiled. "I'm glad he was here to help you."

Eleni focused on Melody. "You look sad."

David felt Melody stiffen beside him. He spoke before she had a chance. "It's been a tough few weeks for us."

"You should stick around here, then. Matthew tends to show up when people is hurting." She looked over David's shoulder. "My dad wants me. Have a good lunch!"

David watched her skip away before turning back to Ryan. "Matthew?"

"He's an angel."

"Angel?" said David. "Like a good person, or like heavenly host, wings, and halos?"

"Well, no one's seen any wings or signs of a halo, but he's shown himself a few times and mysteriously disappeared."

"You really believe the stories?" David smiled slightly with raised eyebrows.

"I'd probably be skeptical too." Ryan reached for his buzzing cell phone and looked at the caller display. "But one of the people he appeared to was me."

Ryan flipped open the phone. "Hey, Britt!"

David sat, not sure what to think about what Ryan had

just shared. He looked at Melody, and she seemed to share his disbelief.

"Have you called Pete? We're on the way!" He slammed the phone shut and stood. "Sorry to interrupt lunch, but I've got to get to the clinic. Something's wrong with my sister."

CHAPTER 16

*M*ELODY KEPT UP WITH RYAN AND David's rushed steps on the two-block walk to the clinic. Ryan burst through the door, and the receptionist immediately called out, "Exam Room 2."

Ryan led the way down a short hall. Crossing to the bedside near Brittany, he said, "What's going on?"

"I'm feeling fine now," said Amber. Her dark hair spilled across a folded blanket, and her short frame almost fit on the exam table without her bending her knees.

Brittany checked her watch. "We'll see what your blood pressure looks like in seven more minutes."

"It spiked?" said Ryan.

"It was 156 over 92 when Mom brought her in," said Brittney.

"I just felt a headache coming on," said Amber.

"Dear, you were pale as winter and having trouble standing," said an older, blond-haired woman on the opposite side of the bed from Ryan. Faye's presence gave Ryan some comfort, as he knew Amber loved and honored her mother-in-law as much as she did their own mom.

"Where's Dr. Williams?" said Ryan.

"He's with another patient," said Brittany. "He said to get her resting on her left side and check it again in twenty minutes."

Ryan looked at Melody. "Everyone, you remember David and Melody."

"Oh, Melody," said Faye, coming over to hug her. "It's good to see you again."

Melody felt the hug all the way to her core. This woman was physically about as different from her mom as she could be, standing equal to Melody in height but doubling her in weight.

Faye pulled back and looked into Melody's eyes. "I was so sorry to hear about your baby."

Melody's voice caught in her throat. "Thank you."

Faye looked toward David. "How long do you get to stay?"

"For a while," said David. "I took some leave in combination with what the commander gave me, so I don't have to report back to Bragg until November twenty-first."

"Good," said Faye. "That's a nice break that I'm sure you both need right now. Are you going to spend all that time here?"

Melody couldn't help but watch Amber lying obediently still on her left side as David and Faye talked.

"We don't have any definite plans, but at some point we'll need to get Melody's mom's car back to her."

Brittany was taking Amber's blood pressure again. Ryan looked at the reading. "Where's Peter?"

"I'm here." He pushed through David and Melody, excusing himself, then apparently recognized who they were. "Oh, hey! Good to see you." His focus was immediately back on his wife lying on the barely propped up exam table.

"Her blood pressure has gone up," said Ryan.

"Okay," said Peter. "What's that mean?"

"It means we're concerned about pregnancy-induced hypertension that could lead to preeclampsia," said Ryan. "Neither is good for the baby, and both would force us to deliver early."

"So what do we do?" said Peter.

"Let's see..." Ryan referred back to the notes Brittany had been making on the chart. "You're thirty-three weeks, four days. Pete, get her home and in bed. Amber, you can get out of that bed to go to the bathroom, but that's it. Nothing else. And lie on your left side as much as possible. Got it?"

"But..." said Amber.

"No," said Ryan, putting up a hand. "I may be your baby brother, but I will absolutely pull doctor rank on you. Whatever else is going on in that brain of yours needs to stop. Your job is to be a mother to that baby, and right now, he needs to you lie in bed. Period."

Brittany touched her shoulder. "Don't worry. We'll all step in and do whatever needs done. Pops can finish getting the furniture set up, Mom and I can take turns helping around the house. You know Heather will come down and help."

Melody watched Amber smile and lie her head back. The family was circling the wagons like she'd seen them do before. The grandfather, even the brother and sister-in-law who lived in Portland would do whatever was necessary to be available once the need was made known. *Why couldn't I have that? Why do I have to be separated from everyone, living by myself on the other side of the country?*

"This doesn't sound like it's for a few days," said Amber.

"We'll see," said Ryan. "I'll stop by tonight and check on you. If you're pressure is still elevated and you're still having the headache or other symptoms, then you're probably going to be in bed for the duration."

"What's the critical point?" said Peter. "I know thirty-three weeks is too early. Is thirty-eight weeks where we need to be?"

"Chances improve exponentially with each week. The next few weeks are critical for his brain, gut, and lungs. Another week and a half would make a huge difference. Every day we can make it past thirty-four weeks will only increase his chances."

"And when she goes into labor?" said Peter.

"Straight to Portland. Baby boy will need more support than we can give him here. We can always call Chief Donovan at the Gilbert Fire Station in Portland if we need ambulance support. He could meet us on 26, part-way into town."

"Sounds like a plan," said Peter. He turned and leaned close to his wife's face. "How are you feeling now?"

"I feel fine. Really. My head's just aching a little."

"No chances, my Ray."

Melody wondered at the endearment. She'd heard it before when she came down for Ryan and Brittany's wedding and had learned then that it had something to do with Amber being Peter's ray of sunshine. *Does David have something he calls me? Normally he just calls me Mel. That doesn't count.*

"David," said Ryan, "outside that door, to your left and down a bit, there should be a wheelchair."

"Ryan," protested Amber, "I can walk to the car."

Ryan pointed at Peter. "No chances, remember?"

David rolled it in, and Peter helped Amber into it.

"I'll bring dinner over tonight along with what we purchased today in town, dear," said Faye.

"Sounds good, Mom," said Peter.

"And everyone else can come for dinner at our house," said Faye. "You too." Faye grabbed Melody's hand and looked deeply into her eyes. "I'd love it if you would come as well."

"Thank you," said Melody. "That's very nice."

Melody walked behind the crowd as Peter rolled Amber out and placed her in his Jeep. She wasn't sure her family would show the open concern for someone like she saw here. *But Mom and Aunt Patricia did fly out when Cole was transferred to Duke. Would I care that much over something in Aunt Patricia's life?*

Ryan held the door open as Brittany rolled the wheelchair back into the clinic. They stopped near her and David.

"Sorry about lunch," said Ryan.

"That's okay," said David. "Maybe next time, we'll actually get to eat."

Ryan looked at Melody for a moment. "Do you really want to come out to Frank and Faye's tonight for dinner?"

"Yeah," said Melody. "I think I do."

Brittany put an arm around her shoulders. "It's good to see you again. Even if I hate the reason for the trip, I'm thankful you're here."

Melody looked back at her, her eyes filling with tears for the first time in almost a week. "Thanks."

CHAPTER 17

*D*AVID REACHED OUT AND GRABBED Melody's hand as they walked back to her aunt's house. "What are you thinking?"

"Hmmm? Oh," she shrugged. "I don't know that I can put it into words. My mind's a jumble right now."

"I was worried that maybe watching everything going on with Amber might be too much."

"It's definitely touching on some raw nerves. I keep wondering what will happen if she does go into labor. It's not like they're close to a hospital here. It's got to be like an hour drive to Portland."

"Probably."

"What if the baby is born too soon? Or they release it from the NICU and something happens later?"

"Like what happened with Cole."

Melody just nodded her head and took a deep breath. They walked for a short while in silence before she said, "I feel different here."

"Different how?"

"They all care about each other so much. But they don't make me feel like an outsider, either."

"I know what you mean. It's like they pull you in, but you don't realize it."

"I wish we had that."

David sighed. Letting go of her hand, he wrapped his arm around her shoulders. "Should I get out of the Army and move us back here?"

Melody paused for a moment. "And what will you do in Crossing?"

"I don't know," he shrugged.

They walked up the driveway, and David saw Patricia sitting on the porch.

"Enjoy your lunch?" she called out.

"We never got to eat," said David.

"How about I go make us some sandwiches as you explain?" said Melody.

She went inside while David sat in a rocker near Patricia and updated her on Amber's status.

"So you're going to eat at Faye's tonight?" said Patricia.

"That's the plan," said David. "Do you mind?"

"Oh, heavens no, child. Go enjoy yourself. I do hope things turn out well for Amber and that baby. Heaven knows the girl's been through quite a lot."

Melody came back outside with a tray covered with two sandwiches, a bunch of grapes, and two glasses of water. "What do you mean?"

"How much has Ryan told you about her?" said Patricia.

"When we were in high school," said David, "I didn't even know he had a sister who was still alive. He barely talked about the one who died."

"Yes, well apparently, when that girl died, the family fell apart. Amber finally ran away from home when she was sixteen. Ryan would have been just about twelve at the time."

"We didn't meet until he was 16," said David.

"In her years on the road," said Patricia, "she survived one pretty decent dog attack and escaped one abusive fellow, both of which put her in the hospital."

"Amber?" said Melody.

Patricia nodded her head. "And that's not to mention the variety of places she slept and despicable places she worked in order to earn enough money to eat semi-regularly."

"I guess I just never thought about it," said Melody. "I knew Brittany had mentioned Amber had been on her own for awhile, but I just never took the time to think about what that might mean. I guess I just thought she was a lot like me."

David shook his head. "She's quite incredible. Looking at her now, I would have never guessed any of that."

"Most people," said Patricia, "have a past touched by tragedy of some kind."

David watched Patricia as her mind seemed to leave the porch and travel back in time. "Sounds like a good story there."

Patricia refocused on him. "Don't know about good, but it's a story. I might even tell it to you one day."

David finished the last bite of his sandwich while thinking about this interesting woman before him. As far as he knew, she'd never married. *Yet she'd carved out a life for herself and remained true to her roots. Or did she? Was Crossing where she and Melody's mom had grown up?* He could recall some family stories, but not any locations.

"Well, you two enjoy the scenery out here," said Patricia. "I'm going to go put together a meal Peter can store in the freezer until they need it."

Patricia went inside, and David looked around at the neatly kept yards and fall flowers in their final colors before the coolness of winter took them. "It really is pretty..." He froze, all his senses heightened.

"Yes, it is," Melody replied.

"Do you see that?"

"What?"

"There," he pointed across the street, one house down. A man stood watching them. Not really close, yet David felt like he could see him as clearly as if he'd been standing inches away. "Blue jeans, white shirt, blue jean jacket, blond hair, and blue eyes."

"Blue eyes? Where are you looking? How on earth can you see what color his eyes are?" Melody stood to look, and David quickly stepped to her side.

"Wait." He looked again but saw no one. "Where did he go?"

Melody raised her eyebrows. "I didn't see anyone, honey. Are you sure it's just not everything catching up with you?"

David scanned the street, taking in every bush or tree where the man could have darted. "Maybe."

THE SUN WAS SINKING LOW IN THE SKY AS DAVID FOLLOWED Ryan's car into Frank and Faye's driveway.

"Do they all live in log houses?" said Melody, looking at the beautiful two-story home with a three-car garage.

"Wow," said David. "Maybe I should go into lumberjacking."

They stepped out and followed Ryan and Brittany inside.

"I'm so glad you all came," said Faye, taking time to hug each one. "You remember Frank?"

Melody took in Frank's tan and weathered face that seemed quick to smile.

"Of course," said David. "It's good to see you again, sir."

Frank extended his hand to David for a shake before

waving them farther into the room. "Come on in and have a seat."

Ryan sat on the leather chair closest to the fireplace while Brittany sat on the ottoman in front of him, leaving the couch to David and Melody. Faye sat beside Melody, and Frank sat in the chair opposite them.

"So tell me," said Faye, "how are you doing?"

"Better, I think," said Melody.

"Well, I can tell you," said Faye, "in the beginning, some days are easier than others, and gradually over time, even the bad days aren't so bad."

"You sound like you are speaking from experience," said David.

"Oh, yes," said Faye, nodding. "We lost our Jamie when she was just ten years old. I really struggled for a long time."

Ten years old! thought Melody. "How did you get through that?"

"One day at a time, dear. Sometimes, one moment at a time. It wasn't easy, but I had to decide that just because God called her home didn't mean He was done using me. Her purpose might be fulfilled, but mine was not."

Melody hadn't really thought about God calling Cole home. Her first thoughts had always been of God taking him from her. Could she be missing something? "How could you see purpose in her death?"

A timer went off in the kitchen. "I've got it, Mom," said Brittany.

Faye took hold of Melody's hand. "I'm not saying I understand it or that I liked it. I was very angry with God for a long time. But then one day I was reading in the book of Job. After God had allowed Satan to test Job by taking almost everything he had, including his children, he started talking, saying things I identified with, like 'Why did I not perish at birth?'"

"Didn't he have friends come to him who only made him feel worse?" said Melody.

"Yes," said Faye. "They were convinced that it was some sin that Job was hiding that had brought all that tragedy on him. But Job was steadfast. Finally, God answered Job and asked him some very important questions. Job realized that God is in control of all things, even the things that seem most out of His control.

"I'm not saying you have to like everything God does," said Faye, "but if you can manage to trust that He is looking out for your best interests, looking out for Cole's best interests, then accepting His plan is a bit easier."

CHAPTER 18

*M*ELODY WAS QUIET ON THE WAY home, and her husband let her be. *Faye lost a child. You'd never know by how she acts. Is that the motivation behind keeping the family so tight knit? She doesn't know how long they have together, so she pushes to keep them close while she can?* It seemed logical but yet didn't seem to be the answer.

When they walked in the door, Melody saw Patricia sitting on the couch, reading her Bible just as she had done every evening they'd been in Crossing.

"Did you enjoy yourselves?" Patricia asked.

"Dinner was very good," said David. "Faye said you owe her a lunch."

Patricia smiled. "Yes, it is about that time again."

"Do you two eat together regularly?" said Melody.

"About once every month. She's always been a good friend."

"Did you know her when she lost her child?" said David.

Patricia's eyes darkened. "Yes. That was a rough few months. She even quit going to church for a time."

"What changed?" said Melody.

Patricia sighed. "I suppose you could say she got radical. She decided that God was enough."

"Enough?" said Melody.

"Yes," said Patricia. "Enough. Heaven knows, we don't understand all God plans. But she decided that if He could figure out how to save her miserable self, then He must be big enough to trust with whatever parts of her heart she could manage to give Him. It was a turning point."

"You mean, she started going back to church and all?" said David.

"Well, yes, she did that too. But more than that. She began living what she believed. When she recognized God romancing her, she figured out how to take His love and give to others."

"God romanced her?" Melody wrinkled her nose in confusion.

"Oh, sure. Romance is more than fancy dinners and roses. Romance is all about one person lavishing love on another, drawing them into a closer relationship. For Faye, her home became an open door, her life an open book to everyone God put in front of her. And some of us didn't follow too easily."

"You?" said Melody. "She affected your life?"

Patricia smiled. "In many ways, child. I don't really talk about it much, but I can't say you'd be sitting here if it weren't for Faye putting her nose in places I thought it didn't belong."

"Sounds like we're back to that interesting story," said David.

"Perhaps someday," said Patricia. "But tonight, I'm going to bed. Goodnight, you two."

Melody watched her aunt pad down the hallway, intensely aware that she knew little about the woman.

"Ready for bed?" said David.

"You go on. I want to sit out here for a little while."

"You want company?"

"No, I'll be fine."

David reached for her hand and gently kissed the top. "I love you."

She smiled at her dear husband. *He's a treasure.* "I love you too."

After he quietly closed the door behind him, she glanced at her aunt's faded Bible. She opened to the book of Job and began to read.

In the land of Uz there lived a man whose name was Job. This man was blameless and upright; he feared God and shunned evil. He had seven sons and three daughters, and he owned seven thousand sheep, three thousand camels, five hundred yoke of oxen and five hundred donkeys, and had a large number of servants. He was the greatest man among all the people of the East.

MELODY STOOD AT THE TOP OF A HILL, WATCHING THREE children play in the field below. A woman ran with them, twirling and laughing. Melody longed to join them but held back.

The woman turned and looked to her. She beckoned, yet Melody hesitated.

She looked behind her and saw Cole nestled in the arms of a man she didn't know, his focus completely on her child. Uncertain, she called to the man, and he looked at her. His blue eyes seemed to pierce her heart, and she gasped.

"I've been here before."

"Yes, Chosen One."

"Are you the angel of death?"

"That is not what this is about."

Tears began to fall down Melody's cheeks. "Did you escort Cole to God?"

"That also is not what this is about."

"I don't... I don't know what you want."

"You cannot move forward by focusing back."

"But he was my heart."

"He was your idol."

Melody gasped. "Is that why God took him from me?"

"No, Chosen One."

"Why do you keep calling me Chosen One?"

"Because it is what you are."

"Chosen? To do what?"

"To go forth."

"Where?"

"Go forth, Chosen One. Complete the task given to you."

Melody sat up, startled awake. She looked about her, dazed. The Bible still lay open in her lap.

"Melody?"

David stood near her. She tried to focus, but the dream was still so vivid in her mind.

"Mel? Are you okay?" He sat down on the couch beside her.

"Yeah. I—" *What? What was that?* "I think...I was just dreaming."

"Want to tell me about it?"

Melody took a deep breath. "I was standing on a hillside, talking to a man who was holding Cole."

David sat back, extending his arm to his wife. Melody cuddled into him.

"Someone we know?" said David.

"No, I've never seen him before. I'm not even sure I could describe him, other than his eyes. They were extreme, like a blue you only see in pictures."

"Blue? With blond hair?"

"Yeah, maybe."

"I thought you didn't see him!"

Melody shifted to look at her husband. "The guy in my dream?"

"The man outside. Remember the man I saw down the street?"

"I didn't see him. Do you think...?"

"What?"

Melody wasn't sure she could voice it out loud. "Maybe Ryan talking about an angel in Crossing just planted a thought in our heads."

"Then why are we both seeing a blond-haired, blue-eyed man?"

"Do you remember how Ryan described him?"

David paused. "I'm not sure."

Melody sat quiet for a moment.

"Why was he holding Cole?" said David.

"I don't know. In my dream I asked him if he was the angel of death, but he said that wasn't the right question."

"What was the right question?"

"I don't know. He said I was chosen to go forth."

"Go forth? Where?"

"That's what I asked."

"Did he give you an answer?"

"Not really. He said I'm supposed to complete the task given to me. He acted like I should know what that meant." Melody shook her head. "I don't have any idea what to do. Could he really have been an angel? Do they appear in both dreams and on streets?"

"I don't know, Mel. Maybe we need to talk to Ryan some more."

"Maybe."

"Why don't you come to bed? It's really late."

"Okay." She glanced back at what she'd been reading. One part sprang off the page at her: *What is mankind that you make so much of them, that you give them so much attention, that you examine them every morning and test them every moment? Will you never look away from me, or let me alone even for an instant?*

CHAPTER 19

*D*AVID FOLLOWED PATRICIA'S DIRECTIONS and pulled onto the road that would lead to the logging office Monday morning.

They'd spent a quiet weekend with Melody's aunt, and he'd watched as Melody was drawn more and more into the Bible. He'd rarely seen his wife pick it up even though they had gone to church most Sundays before his last deployment. Now it seemed like it was becoming a lifeline.

As the office came into view, he saw that it too was a log cabin, although simpler than either of the family's homes they'd already seen. Two storied, it looked like the bottom level was just a large open area with a concrete floor built for machine storage.

"I'm guessing it's up those stairs," said David.

Melody looked around. "I think you're right."

They walked up the stairs and opened the door. The open space looked like barely controlled chaos. Faye looked up from the middle of a paper-strewn desk.

"Hey there!" Faye smiled broadly.

"Hey," said Melody.

"How's it going?" said David.

"Well," Faye looked around her. "To be honest, I'm getting there, despite what this mess might convey. Truth be told, I've been backing out of the office the last couple years, letting Amber take on more and more. Now I'm realizing how much she's been doing and how much I've forgotten!"

"Do you need some help?" Melody asked.

"I'd be grateful for it," said Faye. "But let's eat lunch first."

Faye grabbed a couple of containers out of the refrigerator and added them to a picnic basket. "I thought I'd share one of my favorite spots in Crossing with you."

She handed the basket to David, put on her jacket, and reached for a blanket. David and Melody followed her down the stairs and to a worn path.

"Our house is just through there," said Faye, "and Peter and Amber's is just over that way a bit."

"How is Amber doing?" said Melody.

"She's obeying the doctor's orders fairly well, but she's starting to go a little stir crazy, lying in bed all the time." Faye looked at Melody. "On Wednesday, her mom, Brittany, and I are going to go have lunch with her. I'd love for you to join us."

Melody stayed quiet for a moment, and David tensed as he waited for her answer. *Say yes, Mel.*

Faye reached out and touched her arm. "It's okay if you aren't ready."

They reached a spot with a small clearing near a stream trickling over a gathering of rocks. David put the basket down and walked closer to the water. *Deep enough in some spots to get decently wet, but not flowing quickly enough to make crossing difficult.*

He turned back to the ladies, who had laid out the blanket and were pulling food from the basket. "This is quite a spot."

"Yes," said Faye. "God and I have had a lot of great conversations out here. Sometimes I do most of the talking, and sometimes He does. But it's always good."

Melody handed David a plate. "I really like that bench seat," she said.

Faye smiled. "That was a Christmas present from Peter the year before he and Amber got married."

Melody read the carving in the wood on the back of the bench. *"The LORD has chosen you to be his treasured possession. Deuteronomy 14:2."*

Faye smiled. "That was one of the verses that helped bring my heart some healing after Jamie died."

"What else helped you?" said David.

"Oh, friends who didn't leave me helped, but mostly I think just time. Although...God did give me a bit of a reality check." Faye sat back with a full plate and took a bite of her ham sandwich before continuing. "One of the things that most bothered me was that it seemed God didn't care what I thought about His plan to take Jamie home to Him. As time passed and I'd worked through the worst of my anger, He began to show me places in the Bible where other women had lost their children."

Faye poured a glass of lemonade into a plastic cup while she continued. "Sometimes the death of a child was because of the sins of his parents or their culture. Think of all the babies who died in Egypt during the tenth plague when the Pharaoh would not release the Israelites. Did any of those Egyptian women hold onto anger?"

Faye took a drink. "Or David and Bathsheba's first child. The Lord sent Nathan to tell him their son would die because David showed utter contempt for the Lord when he called Bathsheba to him and then later killed her husband. What would it be like living with a man whose sin caused the death of your child?"

"It doesn't seem fair that our children should pay for our sins," said Melody.

David thought about some of the things he had seen on deployments. "But evidence of that exact thing is all over the world," said David. "Regimes are created on hate, and men spend decades fighting because two brothers had an argument. Or one man grabs for a little power and passes the thirst for control onto his children, who then must have greater power."

"Very true," said Faye. "But God also showed me that sometimes He takes people home to Him for a greater purpose. I think of Mary, the mother of Jesus. She got to love and enjoy him for thirty years, then watched him tirelessly serve others before dying a horrible death."

"But Cole wasn't Jesus," said Melody, tears in her eyes.

"No, he wasn't," said Faye. "And I can't speak to what God's thinking in all this. But as I look back on my Jamie, I can tell you that through her death, I changed. And I don't know that I would have allowed God to change me into the person you see today if I hadn't gone through all that. Not that I was a bad person, mind you. But I wasn't becoming the woman God made me to be."

"So God took her to change you?" said Melody.

"No, not exactly. But because He did take her home, my heart was finally in a place where I was ready to listen more closely to Him." Faye thought for a moment. "I don't know if that makes sense."

David thought about all Faye said. "You're talking about the good that can come from the bad."

"Yes," said Faye. "Our enemy wants to do us harm, but God always has a greater plan. Not everything is good, but God can help us find good because of, or maybe in spite of, the bad."

He'd already considered that, with the heart problems

they now knew Cole would be facing, perhaps death was the easier course for all of them. *But could God be looking at something deeper? Are Mel and I not doing what we were meant to do?*

"Faye," said Melody, "have you ever heard Ryan talk about an angel?"

David's eyes flew to his wife. Her eyes were down, and she picked at a loose thread in the blanket.

"You mean Matthew?"

David looked at Faye. "He's talked about it with you, then?"

"Oh, Ryan's not alone in having seen Matthew. Peter's seen him. Andy, Peter's best friend, has talked to him in person and on the phone. Amber's parents met with him multiple times when they were still looking for her."

"So, he's a real person?" said David.

"I don't believe so. Not like you and me. When Ryan saw him, he was still in bed asleep. He disappeared completely on Peter. And then there's the card thing."

"Card thing?" said Melody.

"Andy is an attorney with an office in town. Matthew stopped by there one day saying he was looking for a girl who met Amber's description. Andy didn't give him any information, but Matthew gave him a card so he could contact him if Andy ever saw the girl. After Andy checked everything out and met with all of us, he called Matthew to set up a meeting with Amber and her parents."

"Wouldn't that make him a human being?" said David.

"Well, later the next day after the reunion, Amber asked Andy for Matthew's number so she could call and thank him."

"The card was gone?" said Melody.

"No, it was different," said Faye. "All the contact information was gone, and under his name was a Bible verse, the one in Hebrews that talks about people entertaining angels unaware."

David met Melody's eyes. Part of him wanted to believe an angel was ministering to them in their pain. *But do angels really appear to people these days?*

"Why do you ask?" said Faye.

"David thought he saw him on the street, but I didn't see anything. I thought maybe his mind was still being hyperactive from being in Afghanistan."

"But then Mel had a dream," said David.

"And he told me things along the lines of what you've been saying," said Melody.

"Lots of times when God is trying to get a message to you," said Faye, "He will confirm it. Sometimes, it's through the Bible; sometimes, through a friend."

"And sometimes through dreams?" said Melody.

Faye patted her hand. "And sometimes through dreams."

CHAPTER 20

TWO DAYS LATER, MELODY MET Faye at the logging office, and they drove together to Peter and Amber's home. Because of the family attraction to log cabins, this time she was expecting the beautiful log home before her.

Brittany opened the front door for them, and Melody looked across an open living and dining room interrupted only by a spiral staircase going up into a loft. Amber was comfortably lying on her side on the couch while an older woman was lighting a cinnamon-vanilla scented jar candle on the coffee table.

"Oh, how pretty," said Faye.

"Victoria thought we could all use a touch of fall," said Brittany.

A chocolate brown tablecloth was folded in half to cover the coffee table, and bright orange leaves encircled the tan-colored candle. Plain white plates sat beside crystal goblets.

"Just because we are eating in the living room," said Victoria, "doesn't mean we have to give up the things that make the dining room pretty."

Victoria walked over to Melody and wrapped one arm around her shoulders. "It's good to see you again. I'm so glad you decided to come."

Amber and Ryan's mom hadn't changed much since Ryan and Brittany's wedding. Her trim figure and modern clothes still showed her meticulous attitude toward details and caring for herself.

Melody returned her smile. "Thanks."

"Remind me, have you and Amber known each other long?"

Melody shook her head. "We just met at Brittany's wedding."

"Mel and I used to work together at Doernbecher's Children's Hospital," said Brittany.

"That's right," said Victoria with a nod of remembrance.

"Who's in the mood for some chicken?" Faye asked.

"That sounds delicious," said Amber. "What kind did you make?"

"I brought chicken piccata," said Faye.

"Oh, yum," said Brittany as she rubbed her expanding belly. "We're eating good today, baby."

Everyone laughed. A timer dinged, and Victoria moved toward the kitchen. "That should be the pasta."

"Amber, we worked this right!" said Brittany. "You provided the home, I provided the salad, and the moms provided the good food!"

Victoria laughed. "Have you always thought with your stomach, Brittany?"

"Always!" said Faye, joining in the laughter.

The women gathered around the food. "Well, let's pray and eat," said Faye. "Father, thank you for the beautiful fall you painted in the trees outside. Help us not to take it for granted. We ask that you continue to heal Melody's heart and bless the growth of Amber's and Brittany's babies. Protect them and use them. Bless this food and help us to become the women you want each of us to be. In Jesus' name, amen."

Faye took the wrapping off the platter of chicken, while Victoria began filling the glasses with lemonade.

"Thank you, guys, for coming over today," said Amber.

"Getting tired of Peter's company?" said Brittany, smirking as she took a bite of chicken.

"No," said Amber with a twinkle in her eye. "But different company is nice. Plus, I think he was going about as stir crazy as I am." Amber laid her head down on her pillow.

"His dad is sure missing him being around," said Faye. "And we miss you horribly in the office. I don't know what kind of mess we're making for you, but I even had poor Melody in there Monday trying to put together end-of-quarter stuff for Allie."

"It wasn't that bad," said Melody with a wave of her hand. "Of course, I don't know what it normally looks like."

Brittany laughed. "If it was anything like Mom's normal creative process, I bet the office looked like a tornado went through."

"Now girls, some of us have different systems." Victoria winked at Faye as she continued. "I frequently think that the more that is dragged out during the cleaning process, the neater it will be in the end."

"Yes," said Brittany, "but how near the end are we?"

"Well," said Faye. "I suppose we'll find out when Allie gets back to me tomorrow. And when Amber gets back to work."

"Are you missing it, Amber?" asked Melody.

"Hmm?" Amber squinted at Melody and tried to prop herself up a little, pausing immediately after she began moving.

"Amber?" said Faye, looking alert.

Brittany got off the floor and went to Amber's side. "What is it? What are you feeling?"

Eyes closed, Amber lay very still. "My head really hurts. The light is bothering my eyes, and I feel nauseous."

Brittany looked at Victoria. "Do you know where the blood pressure cuff is?"

Victoria went to the bedroom.

Melody felt Faye's hand on her arm. She looked at her and gave her best attempt at a smile. *God, I don't know why you took Cole, but I'm asking that you don't take Amber's baby.*

Victoria handed the cuff to Brittany. The room stilled, waiting for Brittany's response.

"Mom, call Ryan and Peter. We've got to get her to Portland."

THE NEXT SEVERAL MINUTES WERE A FLURRY OF ACTIVITY AS Victoria found Amber's hospital bag and Brittany prepared Amber for travel. Peter rushed in the door and was promptly sent out to his Jeep with pillows and a blanket to try to make the trip as comfortable as possible for Amber.

By the time Ryan arrived, they were ready to go. Peter carried Amber out, and Ryan helped to maneuver her into the back seat with Peter.

"Roll left as much as you can, sis," said Ryan.

Doors were shut, and Ryan jumped in the driver's seat, while Brittany hopped in the front passenger seat. Then they raced away.

As soon as they were off, Victoria grabbed her purse. "I'm going to stop in town and get Thomas, then head to Portland."

Melody hadn't met Amber's father yet but imagined him to be soft-spoken like his wife.

At the door, Victoria paused and looked back at Faye. "Are you going to come up? Or do you want me to call you?"

"Call me," said Faye. "We'll come up once she's resting in her room."

"Okay," said Victoria, shutting the door behind her as she hurried off to her car.

Faye looked at Melody. "You okay?"

"A little shaky, but I think it's because my mind keeps playing through all the possibilities." Melody shrugged. "I was able to pray for the baby while everyone was getting things ready to go."

"That's my girl." Faye wrapped an arm around her shoulders. "How about we keep praying and get this lunch cleaned up? I figure it will be at least an hour and a half before we hear anything at all. Might as well keep busy."

MELODY RETURNED TO HER AUNT'S HOUSE TO FIND PATRICIA working in the flower garden. "Just tryin' to get these things cleaned up before the snow flies. That termination dust is getting lower on the mountains. Should have some snow before long."

Melody looked toward the mountains, remembering how everyone watched the snow line getting lower on the mountains to judge how much longer before summer "terminated" and the snow started falling in the lower elevations.

"Want some help?"

As they worked side-by-side, pulling weeds and trimming back plants, Melody filled Patricia in on the events of the afternoon.

Patricia sat back for a moment in the grass. "Well, I guess we'll know God's choice soon."

"Are you worried?"

"No sense in doin' that quite yet, child."

"Do you worry about anything, Aunt Patricia?"

"Oh, sure."

"What do you do? How do you keep your worries under control?"

Patricia shrugged. "I pray."

"Pray. It's that simple?"

"Well, simple, yes. Never confuse simple with easy."

The words reverberated within Melody's head. *Never confuse simple with easy.*

"Reading your Bible every day is a discipline. It's simple, but not always easy because life gets busy, or you get sick, or whatever. Prayer is also a discipline, and with practice, it becomes more natural. The more you tell yourself to pray over every little worry, the easier it is to do it before you think about it. It becomes part of your brain's programmed response, like riding a bike or driving a car."

The front screen door slammed shut, and David strode into view. "Mel, Faye just called. She said to call her back when you have a moment, but Amber gave birth to a healthy baby boy."

CHAPTER 21

*M*ELODY GAVE DAVID A BIG HUG just before rushing inside to wash her hands so she could return Faye's call.

"Hi, Faye."

"Oh, Melody. I knew you'd want to know. Little Daniel is doing great. Peter said he weighed in at four pounds twelve ounces, which is too small for the regular nursery. So they'll keep him in the NICU. Also, the hospital wants to hang onto him until thirty-five weeks just to be on the safe side, but right now he looks strong."

Melody breathed a sigh of relief. "When does he reach thirty-five weeks?"

"Saturday, and Amber should be released on Friday, so that works out just about perfect."

"Are Peter and Amber going to stay in Portland until the baby is released?"

"Yes. Our oldest son, Logan, and his family live just this side of Portland. They'll stay there until Daniel can come home."

"I'm so glad things are going well."

"Me too, dear," said Faye.

Melody hung up the phone and felt a prick to her heart. *Oh, Cole.*

David came up behind her. "You okay?"

She looked up and smiled at him. "The baby's name is Daniel. He's little but looks good. They are hoping he'll get to come home Saturday."

"Do you want to go see him?"

Melody thought about walking back into a hospital. Her mind argued back and forth. *It's a different hospital, but it's still a NICU. Daniel is doing well, but the baby next to him might not be.*

As she ran through the debate, her eyes focused on her aunt standing just inside the front door. "What do you think, Aunt Patricia?"

"I think I didn't just bury my own baby less than a month ago."

"Should I go?" Her eyes pleaded with her aunt.

"Child, if you go, go out of a love for Amber. If you don't go, know that everyone in that family understands. They aren't askin' or expectin' a single thing from you except that which you can willingly give."

Melody groaned and sat down on the couch. "I think that makes this harder."

David sat beside her. "There's no rush. We don't have to be back in North Carolina for two more weeks. Let's take it easy tonight and see what you think tomorrow."

By lunchtime Thursday, Melody had made up her mind.

"David, I want to go visit Amber," she had said as they sat around the kitchen table.

Patricia had shooed them out of the house, telling them

she was fully capable of cleaning up the dishes. Now, as Melody looked up at the large white building that housed Oregon Health & Science's children's hospital, she wasn't sure this was a good idea.

David parked the car. "Are you ready?"

Melody inhaled deeply. "I'm not sure I can go see the baby."

"That's fine."

"What-if" questions began to torment her mind. "What if I can't do this?"

"Then we go back to Crossing."

"But what if I start to cry in Amber's room?"

"Then I'll hold you."

"But what if..."

"Mel. Stop." David reached for her hand. "The only way we're going to know what will happen is if we get out of this car and walk into the hospital. We don't have to be here. We can turn and walk away at any moment."

She gazed deeply into his eyes.

"Okay?" he said.

"Okay."

They walked into the building hand-in-hand and made their way to Amber's room. David softly knocked, and Melody opened the door slightly. "Can we come in?"

Peter grinned. "Hey! It's good to see you guys."

Melody slipped over to the bed and hugged Amber.

"I'm so glad you came," said Amber, her eyes tearing.

"I wanted to see you," said Melody.

"How's everything going?" said David.

"Good," said Peter, offering Melody his seat. "Although he's having ... what is it called, Ray?"

"Phototherapy," said Amber. "He was developing some jaundice, so they put him under the light to help."

"How long does he have to be under that?" Melody asked.

"Should just be a couple of days," said Amber.

"It will probably postpone his release a day or two," said Peter.

Melody fidgeted in the chair. "Daniel is a great name."

"Thanks," said Amber. "He's named after his grandfather and father."

Peter offered more of an explanation. "The tradition in my family—started by our Danish ancestors—is that each baby accepts a name from one of its grandparents. My dad's name is Franklin Daniel."

"And I wanted him to have a piece of his daddy," said Amber.

"But I refused to let her consider my middle name!" said Peter, winking at his wife.

"So, it's Daniel Peter?" said David.

Peter nodded.

Amber looked at Melody. "I don't know whether to ask you or not..."

Melody's breath caught in her throat, and she could feel her heart pounding.

"Do you want to go see him?" said Amber.

The concern in Amber's face was almost overwhelming, and tears began gathering in Melody's eyes.

"You don't have to," said Peter. "If it's too much..."

David knelt beside his wife. She met his gaze as she wiped tears from her cheeks and then glanced at Amber, who was also crying.

"Melody," said Amber, "I'm so sorry. I shouldn't have asked..."

"No, please don't be sorry," said Melody. "I just... I just don't know if I'll be able to handle going into the NICU."

"Please don't feel pressured," said Amber. "I'm just so glad you came."

"Will you think less of me if I say yes, but then can't go in?" said Melody.

"Not if you don't think less of me when you watch me try to get out of this bed," said Amber, smiling.

Melody smiled back. "Want to know the trick I learned?"

Melody helped Amber out of bed and into her robe while the guys waited in the hallway. As Amber led the way, Melody focused on putting one foot in front of the other. They paused at the NICU doors, and Amber looked at Melody.

"Are you okay?" said Amber.

"So far," said Melody.

Amber walked through the doors, and Melody took a deep breath. Trailing behind, she tried to keep her eyes focused on Amber, but the babies drew her eyes.

Some lay in plastic isolettes, some in open beds. Some had ventilators, many had IV bags, and all of them had monitors with flashing numbers. She had learned so much in the last year as she recognized the meaning behind some of the numbers on the monitors.

"Hey, folks," said a nurse. "It's not quite time to feed your baby again, is it?"

"No," said Peter. "We had some friends stop in for a visit."

"Ever been in a NICU before?" said the nurse.

Melody didn't trust her voice to speak clearly, so she just nodded. David put his arm around her shoulders.

"You okay?" said the nurse.

"We just recently lost our son," said David. "This is a bit overwhelming."

"I'm sorry," said the nurse. "He was in the NICU?"

Melody barely saw David nod through her tears.

"Not here," he explained. "North Carolina."

"Well, feel free to sit and enjoy this little one as long as you like."

The nurse walked away, and Amber grabbed Melody's hand. "Do you need to leave?"

Melody looked at the precious child lying under the phototherapy lamp before her. Aside from the slight yellow color to his skin, he was tiny and beautiful. Dark hair stuck out at odd angles around his head, and one tiny fist stretched out from his side.

Tears flowed freely. "Oh, Amber. He's gorgeous."

CHAPTER 22

*D*AVID HADN'T REALIZED HOW MUCH walking into the NICU would bother him. When he'd rushed home to see Cole, his entire focus has been on his son. Now, as he sat on the front porch of Patricia's home Sunday afternoon, snapshots of what he'd witnessed three days earlier still haunted him.

How did Mel survive all those days in the NICU? Does she still see the wires and hear the monitors?

"Not most of the time."

The voice startled him, and he jumped from the chair, spinning to see its source. Leaning on the porch railing was a blond, blue-eyed man casually dressed in blue jeans and a long-sleeved shirt.

"Matthew?"

He nodded.

"You can read my thoughts?"

"I just repeat what messages come from the Father."

A ruby-crowned kinglet lighted on a tree branch near Matthew, while an orange and white tabby cat climbed the porch steps.

"God's personal messenger," said David.

"Primary job description."

"So what's the message?"

Matthew chuckled. "Nothing like getting to the point, huh?" The tabby cat rubbed against Matthew's leg, and he crouched down to scratch around its ears.

"Angels like small talk?"

Matthew grinned. "You both are gaining fresh perspectives while in Crossing, but the trip home quickly approaches. Don't let the pain of walking back into the home you shared with Cole surprise you."

David squared his jaw. *Going home.* "Okay."

Matthew straightened and leaned against the railing. "Also remember your place."

"My place? What's that mean?"

"When is the last time you read Ephesians?"

David thought. "Apparently, too long ago."

Matthew stayed quiet, watching David's movements.

"Okay," said David. "Maybe I've never read the book in its entirety."

"It's time," said Matthew.

David nodded, and in the blink of an eye, Matthew was gone. The cat meowed at David, flicked its tail, and gracefully trotted down the porch steps.

David stepped inside and saw Melody sitting on the couch reading Patricia's Bible, while Patricia sat on the other end of the couch working in her crossword puzzle book. The women glanced up at him.

He looked at Patricia. "Do you have another Bible around here I can borrow?"

CHAPTER 23

*M*ELODY GRIPPED THE PHONE RECEIVER tighter. "Why aren't they coming home today? I thought the phototherapy was going well and that he would be released this morning."

"When we stopped by yesterday after church," said Brittany, "the plan was to release Daniel this morning. But now they want to run some more tests. Amber said the doctor had some concerns about his hearing."

"What kind of concerns?"

"Not sure. The tests were supposed to be run today, so I'm hoping to hear more tonight."

"We were planning to return to my mom's on Wednesday. Will you let me know how things are going?"

"Absolutely. How are you doing?"

"Better than when I got here, that's for sure."

"Good. Want to do lunch tomorrow before you leave?"

Melody chuckled. "Lunch never seems to work out well for us."

Brittany laughed. "Well, maybe tomorrow will go better."

Melody hung up and sought out her aunt. "Something's

up with Daniel's hearing. They're keeping him another day or two to run some more tests."

"God knows what He's doing," said Patricia.

Melody smiled. "Yes, I believe He does."

Patricia looked at her and just nodded.

THE NEXT DAY, MELODY RUSHED IN THE DINER DOOR AND SAW Brittany sitting in a corner booth. "Sorry! I was trying to get some laundry done before I pack."

"That's okay. Are you ready to go home?"

"Kinda, I guess. I miss having my own space, but I will miss all of you guys too."

"Have you made any friends there?"

"Not really."

"Time to fix that, girl."

"I know. The church we've been going to has a military group. I think I'll start there."

"Sounds like a good plan."

A waitress in a brown-colored apron with little orange pumpkins placed a glass of water in front of Melody and asked if the pair knew what they wanted.

Melody grabbed a menu from behind the napkin container. "Go ahead and order, Brittany. I need just a minute."

"Chef salad today, please."

"Extra turkey?" said the waitress.

"Yeah, thanks."

The waitress turned to Melody.

"I think I'll have the hot turkey sandwich."

"Do you want a pickle and chips?"

"No pickle. Chips are fine."

The waitress hurried away, and Melody asked the question that had consumed her prayers since yesterday.

"Did you hear anything from Peter or Amber?"

"Yes." Brittany leaned back against seat. "Doctors say Daniel has conductive hearing loss."

"What's that mean?"

"Conductive simply refers to the outer or middle ear. They say he definitely has some hearing loss, but they're not sure how much. The doctor ordered some blood work and an MRI."

"An MRI is one of the things that takes pictures, right?"

"Right. It uses radio waves to take pictures of internal organs. Daniel's MRI showed the bones in his middle ear aren't set up quite right. Those are the ones that connect the vibrations of the ear drum to the cells that send the information to the brain."

"Can they do anything to help him? I can't imagine life without sound."

"Well, I'm not sure. I know they do have some artificial replacements that can be effective in patients that are missing bones, but I don't know what the recommendations will be if things just aren't sitting right. The hospital is referring them to a specialist, but otherwise, they should get to come home tomorrow."

Memories of Cole responding to her voice flooded Melody's mind. She could only imagine what Amber must be going through. "I will keep them in my prayers."

"How about you?" said Brittany, leaning back against the seat.

"I'm doing okay, I guess," said Melody.

"What does that mean?"

Melody shifted in her seat as the waitress brought their drinks and both women thanked her. "Aunt Patty said something the other day that stuck with me, something that I had to investigate more. Have you ever thought about the word *romance?*"

"You mean like dates and falling in love?"

"That's all I really thought it was. David would bring me flowers, and we'd go out to a nice dinner and maybe a movie. But when I looked it up in the dictionary, I found out that it means to court the favor of someone."

"That makes sense. David was courting your favor with a nice meal or by spending time and attention on you."

"True. But think deeper than that. David always has an ulterior motive—he courts my favor so that I will love him. That's what God does. He courts our favor so that we will love Him."

Brittany took a drink, pausing before she spoke again. "I can see all that, Melody, but David does things that makes it easy for you to love him. What difference does all this make when you consider what you've been through the last few months?"

Melody twisted the paper wrapper from her straw around her fingers, shaking her head. "I'm not sure I have a good answer to that. A couple times while I was with your mom, she mentioned the book of Job, so I decided to read it."

The waitress reappeared and placed their food on the table. "Do you ladies need anything else?"

Brittany shook her head. "I think we're good. Thanks." The waitress walked away, and Brittany looked at Melody. "Want me to pray over this before you continue so we can eat while we talk?"

Melody nodded, and after Brittany spoke a short prayer, Melody crunched a chip before getting back to Job.

"As I read, I had to admit that I couldn't quite stand before God as boldly as Job did. I saw where I had put my trust in things like money, family, and David. They were my security. But I still wanted to cry out like Job did when he demanded God answer him."

"That's understandable," said Brittany. "It's natural to ask why when something happens like what you've been through."

"I must have read God's reply to Job a hundred times, but one verse stuck with me more than the rest. In chapter 40, God says, 'Do you still want to argue with the Almighty? You are God's critic, but do you have the answers?' (Job 40:2, NLT)"

Brittany played with the straw in her drink. "Wow. So where does that leave you now?"

Melody shrugged. "Trusting that God has the best in mind. At least, I think my head is wrapped around that." Melody looked into Brittany's eyes, tears beginning to form on her lashes. "My heart is still trying to get it."

Brittany covered Melody's hand with her own. "You'll get there."

ONE WEEK LATER, DAVID PULLED INTO THEIR DRIVEWAY AT home. Melody sighed deeply. "I'm so glad we're done traveling," she said.

Both paused and looked at the front door. David reached for her hand. "Ready to go inside?"

She smiled at him. "Yes."

David opened the front door, and Melody walked in, setting the bag she carried down near the couch. She looked about, her eyes resting on the countertop between the living room and kitchen. A small pot of yellow and purple pansies sat surrounded by cards.

Melody walked over and fingered the quiet flowers. The

card attached read, "Please call if you need anything. Lisa." A house key sat on the counter by the pot.

"Lisa?" said David.

"Your team leader's wife. I think we should have them over for dinner. After all she did for us—contacting the chaplain, organizing meals, taking care of the house while we were gone—it's the least we could do."

David wrapped her in a hug. "I like the idea."

While David carried suitcases back to the bedroom, Melody stopped in Cole's doorway. She looked at the room, her heart filled with loss but not overwhelmed. She walked to the crib and let herself remember him peacefully sleeping or quietly cooing.

She looked at the glider where she had last held him before receiving the call to get him to the hospital. Tears crept down her cheeks.

"I miss him, God, but I thank you for the time I had with him."

She heard David enter the room. He walked up behind her and wrapped his arms around her. She leaned back against him, laying her arms on top of his.

He sighed. "So, now what?"

"We unpack and go to bed. Tomorrow we get up."

"And then?"

"And then I plan to do what God told me to do. Go forth, find my purpose, and fulfill it."

He turned her around and looked into her eyes. "Do you know what that is?"

She shook her head. "Not exactly. But what I saw in Crossing—I want that."

"As long as I stay in the Army, family may never live close."

Melody wrapped her arms around David and leaned into his chest. "That's not quite what I mean."

She held on for a moment, and David waited patiently, just holding her as they stood by their baby's crib. Finally she continued. "Faye was able to find peace after losing her daughter. More than that, she found happiness."

She stood up straighter so she could look into David's eyes. "I don't like a lot about the Army, but I've watched you grow and excel at what you do. I believe God made you to do exactly what you are doing. And if I believe God made you to be a warrior, then He made me to be a warrior's bride. Part of my purpose is accepting that and learning how to thrive as an Army wife."

David didn't say a word for a moment. His eyes seemed to be asking how deeply she meant what she'd just said. Melody held his gaze, waiting for his response.

"I love you, Melody Podell."

She smiled at him. "I know. I love you too."

David leaned in and kissed her forehead. Melody hesitated but decided to ask. "Do you know what Matthew meant when he told you not to forget your place?"

"I've probably read Ephesians twenty times in the last week, and there's so much good stuff!"

Melody could feel the excitement growing in him. He leaned away from her slightly as he talked.

"I love the whole part about spiritual armor to protect ourselves from the enemy's attacks. The belt of truth, breastplate of righteousness, the sword of the Spirit. So much of it relates to the same gear I wear in the field that those words just come alive for me.

"But so much of Ephesians is saying that while I've been saved by faith, I must cooperate in my heart's cleaning process. God chose me, and there are great blessings for me, but I still must follow the directions of my Commander-in-Chief." David shrugged. "I'm explaining this badly."

"So reading Ephesians confirms that your place is in the Army?"

"Yeah, but God's Army. Not the United States Army." David released her for a moment and walked towards Cole's crib. He gripped the rails as he gaze fell on the empty bed. "Mel, if it hadn't been for Ryan and his family, how easy would it have been to walk away from God forever?"

She didn't have to think long for her answer. "Very easy."

He turned his head to her. "Exactly. But Faye and Brittany and Amber and all those people in Crossing were on the battlefield, whether they knew it or not, joining forces with your Aunt Patricia and ... and God. They fought for us. We need to honor that. We need to worship God because He sought us out. And we need to find our place on the battlefield to help others who need what we have to offer."

She moved closer and covered his hand that held onto the side of the crib. "I couldn't agree more."

THAT NIGHT, MELODY SLEPT IN HER OWN BED, SNUGGLED against David. In her dreams, she stood at the top of a hill watching three children play in the field below. A woman ran with them, twirling and laughing. Melody longed to join them but held back.

The woman turned and looked to her. She beckoned.

She looked behind her and saw Cole nestled in the arms of Matthew, his focus completely on her child. She called to him.

"Chosen One," said Matthew, "go forth. Complete the task given to you."

Melody turned and looked back at the woman playing with the children. They had fallen to the ground, and the woman scooped the children up in a group hug.

The woman looked up at her, and Melody gasped with recognition. "That's me!" She looked back at Matthew. "Down there. That woman. It's me."

"Yes, Chosen One. You were chosen to be a mother to more than just Cole. Go forth and complete the task given to you."

Melody looked at the baby in Matthew's arms. "I will always love you, Cole."

Then Melody looked at Matthew. "Thank you for helping us through this."

"The glory does not belong to me, but to the One who sent me."

Melody smiled at him before turning back to the woman and children. Slowly, she proceeded down the hill.

CHAPTER 24

*P*ATRICIA ROLLED OVER ON HER side. She was soaked in sweat from the pain, and as soon as the episode ended, she would need to change the sheets.

"Oh, Father," she forced out through clenched teeth. "This one's a doozie. Give me strength."

Breathe, child.

Patricia concentrated all her energy on slow breaths in and out. After what seemed like an hour, the pain began to subside. Slowly, her body relaxed.

She carefully sat up in bed. "Thank you, Father."

She looked at the mess of wet sheets around her. "I think we'll just worry about these tomorrow, Father, since I no longer have guests taking up the other bed."

DID YOU LIKE THE BOOK?

Would you please leave a review with your favorite bookstore or book club?

Want more from Carrie Daws? Check out all the book related Freebies available at CarrieDaws.com. You'll find book club discussion guides, additional short stories, and more!

Want even more? Carrie loves to support and talk with Christian readers! Not only does she personally respond to every email she receives, but she's provided options with you in mind:

A Forum where readers can talk with Carrie
Weekly devotions

Check it out on CarrieDaws.com!

ABOUT THE AUTHOR

God rewrote Carrie's dreams from being a corporate accountant to an author. With a background writing devotions, a mentor encouraged her to think bigger. The writing monster she now barely keeps contained was born.

After ten years in the US Air Force, Carrie's husband medically retired, and they settled in North Carolina. With their three children figuring out what they want to do in life after school, Carrie stays busy keeping up with her family, loving on women, and reading as much as she can.

For more information about Carrie, please visit CarrieDaws.com.

ALSO BY CARRIE DAWS

The Other Crossing Books:
Crossing Values (Book 1)
Ryan's Crossing (Book 2)
Crossing's Redemption

THE EMBERS SERIES
Kindling Embers
Igniting Embers
Extinguishing Embers

THE SACRED TRUST SERIES
Seeking Isabel
Finding Benjamin
Banishing Felipe

HOME FRONT HEROINES SERIES
More Than Meets the Eye
Not My Ways